New Pack Order

Pack #4

Eve Langlais

New York Times Bestselling Author

Copyright © May 2014, Eve Langlais
Copyright © 2nd Edition April 2016
Cover art © Mina Carter, May 2014
2nd Edition Edits by Devin Govaere

Produced in Canada
Published by Eve Langlais
1606 Main Street, PO Box 151
Stittsville, Ontario, Canada, K2S1A3
http://www.EveLanglais.com

ISBN-13: 978 1988 328 28 7

ALL RIGHTS RESERVED

New Pack Order is a work of fiction and the characters, events and dialogue found within the story are of the author's imagination and are not to be construed as real. Any resemblance to actual events or persons, either living or deceased, is completely coincidental.

 No part of this book may be reproduced or shared in any form or by any means, electronic or mechanical, including but not limited to digital copying, file sharing, audio recording, email and printing without permission in writing from the author.

Chapter One

Dim lighting did little for the cavernous room with its arched ceiling, which soared high overhead. The sparse illumination couldn't dispel the shadows, but it did hide the dust nestled in the folds of the floor-to-ceiling, red velvet drapes. Someone was stuck in the Dark ages and in need of an interior decorator, not to mention a better housekeeper.

A good thing Thaddeus had been cured of allergies when he gave up sunlight, else he might have found it hard to sit without sneezing. As it was, an allergic reaction would have proven more exciting than the dull drone of his so-called peers.

Bored with the conversation, Thaddeus drummed his fingers on the carved armrest of the overstuffed chair he sat in, listening to the sleep-inducing buzz of those around him as they endlessly argued the same thing over and over. They never tired of it. Such was the curse of eternity and having all the time in the world to ponder and make decisions. This century was known for quick decisions and a lack of patience.

Would a little speed kill them? It irritated him, which was ironic considering most would count him among one of the eldest ones present. At three hundred and forty-two, he'd long left the days of his youth and humanity behind. But it didn't mean he'd gotten old, or caught in his ways. On the contrary, Thaddeus liked to think he kept up with the times.

As the conversation kept circling around one basic fact, he couldn't take it anymore. "Is it really that important?" he interrupted. "Yes, we all understand that protocol was broken when Roderick meddled in the affairs of the Lycans and then broken again when we reached out to speak to the leader of the pack in trouble."

"We?" Cue the heavy sarcasm. "You mean you. You contacted the dogs and gave them your aid."

Thaddeus snorted. "Aid? I'd hardly call what I did help. I simply led the dogs in the right direction to take care of their problem, which was also our problem. A dilemma, I might add, our former queen created."

Clear blue eyes regarded him from under blond brows. Morpheus pursed his lips. "The law is clear. Under no circumstances are we to contact humans or wolves."

"Not entirely true. If there is strong enough reason, then the council or the current king and queen may contact a high-ranking wolf with the understanding that all said contact is to be kept secret under penalty of death. I didn't tell anyone I called them, except for you, but we're both on the council so that technically doesn't count."

"And what of who the dog told?"

"Do we have proof he blabbed?"

Steam practically simmered from Morpheus's ears. "None we can verify. However, you should have gotten permission first."

"A rapid decision was required, something the council seems incapable of." Thaddeus couldn't help his smirk.

Instead of launching into a verbal tantrum, Morpheus laced his hands behind his back, and his expression smoothed. He even smiled, which Thaddeus didn't trust. "Very well, I will concede that you were within your bounds as a council member to speak to the alpha. However, even you can't deny the other problem. The law has been broken. The dogs know of our existence."

Should Thaddeus point out the obvious? Of course. "The Lycan high council has always known of us."

"Only because of necessity. Everyone below them is supposed to remain ignorant."

Again, he couldn't resist. "Kind of hard to remain ignorant when a vampire is killing them left and right, not to mention experimenting on humans, taking over their minds and making the Lycans into puppets, and doing everything to shine a spotlight on his activities."

And there was the loss of control Thaddeus had striven for.

Morpheus slammed his fists down on the heavy wooden table. "We would have taken care of Roderick."

An arched brow eloquently displayed his

incredulity. "Really? And when were you planning to do this? Once he'd either killed or converted all the Lycans into his own army of darkness? Perhaps after he'd murdered or kidnapped one human too many? The man was a monster. If you ask me, we should be thanking those wolves for handling the problem for us."

A sneer curled Morpheus's lips. "We don't require the help of canines. Filthy creatures."

"Filthy creatures who took down one of the strongest, most dangerous vampires we've ever encountered." It seemed there were reasons behind the laws that said no vampires were to ever attempt to convert Lycans, laws the former queen had willingly broken.

The truth was a sour reminder that put a pucker on more than one face present, not that they spoke out of turn. The vampire council for the North American flocks bowed to Morpheus, letting him speak for them. All that was except Thaddeus. Oddly enough, despite not leading more than a handful of minions, he not only held a seat but was considered one of the more formidable members present in the room.

"Be that as it may, whether helpful or not, we still must take care of them. The wolves must be eliminated."

And they came back to the same debate. The one Thaddeus grew tired of. "Again I ask, why? It's not as if the wolves are going to publicly proclaim our existence. They have their own secret to hide."

Cold blue eyes, old eyes, in a face forever young, pierced Thaddeus, or tried to. As if he could be so easily intimidated. "Do you need a reminder of our laws? Most specifically, the one which states that those who've fallen under the influence of one of our own must either turn themselves over to the control of another or perish when their master does."

A mocking smile tilted his lips. "Are we calling Roderick, that psychotic experiment, one of ours now? Funny, I would have thought the Lycans had first claim."

"The dogs gave him up to our former queen, thus relinquishing all rights to him. And he left behind all his former familial ties when he transformed."

Use the law to support their flimsy excuses? Two could play that game. Thaddeus leaned forward. "Ah, but didn't he forfeit his vampire rights when he murdered his maker and those close to her? Wasn't he a wanted criminal, placing him outside our laws? Since when do those who flout our rules enjoy their protection? What's done is done. The unholy abomination is dead. His murderous rampage halted, his ashes contained, and the wolves are content to live out their lives and forget our existence. So why are we having this ridiculous debate? Hunting down those who succumbed to Roderick's spells will only serve to anger the Lycans and cause war. Is that what you want?"

As soon as he said it, he could sense the truth

and see it in the faces around him. Red light glinted in the irises of a few. Hunger popped the canines of others. And madness, madness tinged with bloodlust, stirred the blood of the rest.

It stunned him, he who thought he'd seen it all. "You want war," he stated. "But why? Why now? Why when the world, make that humanity, is sure to notice? Is it your desire to return to the Dark Ages, where all knew vampires walked the dark shadows of night? To see us hunted until our numbers grow desperately low? It took us decades to recover the last time." And given how many of them burned and had their ashes scattered and taken a part of the collective strength with them.

"As you've stated, the world has changed, and we tire of living in shadows." Morpheus rose and paced before the window with his hands clasped behind his back. The image of a lord from a century or two ago. "We are powerful beings. We should be leading the masses, not hiding from them."

"Then don't live in shadows. There's no need to start a war though."

"Pacifist." The word was spat as an insult.

Once, Thaddeus might have taken insult. Once, he would have challenged the person to a duel—and won. He'd have taken the heart of his rival, ripped it from his chest, pulsing and dripping. He would have devoured it to draw the strength of the winner into his own body. But that was a long time ago. The petty squabbles and power games no longer entertained him. After centuries of living, he'd finally grown up. "Call me what you will, but I will not be a part of this."

"Then leave." Morpheus waved a hand, his gesture dismissive.

A good idea. Thaddeus rose from his seat, his casual attire of jeans and a gray knit sweater surely grating the fashion sense of those stuck in the past with their high-collared, starched shirts, ruffles, and waistcoats. "I shall leave, and I guarantee you, I won't be alone. Once others hear of your foolhardy plan, council or not, you'll find yourselves without the numbers to back you, and when the wolves come to exact their revenge, don't cry for my help."

"Why would we call when we'll already own your strength?"

A threat like that could mean only one thing.

An existence honed by an instinct for survival had Thaddeus ducking before he even heard the whisper of sound that signaled the ambush. Amateurs. He'd not lived to such a ripe old age by not listening to his instincts. Those instincts screamed at him to run.

Before any labeled him cowardly, please note, it was only the dead and foolhardy who remained to fight against untenable odds, and Thaddeus was anything but stupid.

Whisking strands of shadows around him, a skill not all could manage, and thick enough that the younger, lesser-trained vamps couldn't pierce them, he flitted from pillar to pillar, flicks of his fingers sending out jolts of power that popped the incandescent bulbs one by one.

As true dark descended, chaos rose to take its place, but Thaddeus didn't remain to admire his handiwork. With treachery afoot and stalking the halls of the castle, he needed to flee. First, though, he needed to make a stop and grab something. Something he was pretty sure Morpheus wanted. *But he's not getting it.*

Chapter Two

The awful presence in Marc's head vanished. He could have sobbed in relief as it left, the heavy weight forcing him to do its bidding, an evil entity intent on using him to further his murderous agenda. Trapped within his own mind, Marc couldn't even scream for help. He could do nothing, nothing but watch as he betrayed his friends and bear silent witness as he destroyed a burgeoning relationship, cringe in horror as he did unspeakable things and all because of a warped being with a hard-on for revenge and power.

But that had been last night, before the battle between the free wolves and the mind-controlled ones. In the end, good had prevailed. Roderick died, and the rogue wolves got back what was left of their minds, which, in many cases, amounted to not too much. Some died in those first few hours of liberty from fighting amongst themselves, others from suicide—who wanted to live with atrocities on their conscience?—and the rest scattered.

Like many of those freed, his own waking nightmares plagued him.

I could smell her fear and see it in her eyes. The words that spewed from my mouth…How I wanted to scream it wasn't me saying those vile things. Wasn't me grabbing her with an intent to harm.

But Roderick controlled me. A fucking monster took over my body and used me.

Poor Thea, how scared she must have been when I threatened her. If only she'd aimed the gun a little higher and spared me the shame.

But she hadn't and Marc had lived despite his betrayal, and in the end Roderick died, leaving Marc once again free to make his own decisions. Little consolation given what he'd done because he already knew he could never make amends, or forget.

Hiding in the woods, he avoided those searching for survivors. The killing was over, and the cleanup had begun, the offer of healing and a return to the pack extended to those caught by the army of good, a pack ruled by a strong and decent alpha, a pack, once upon a time, he wouldn't have minded becoming part of.

His friends Trent and Darren were part of the good pack. They'd had the strength of mind to resist the insidious whisperings of a mad vampire. Poor beta Marc had succumbed too easily. *Like a fucking loser.* If he'd not worn his wolf shape, he would slap his forehead with a big, fat L.

He heard his friends calling for him, and Marc knew if he showed himself, they'd take him, broken and apologetic, back into the bosom of the pack. They'd even forgive him, those wonderful bastards. But there would always be those who looked at him with distrust. He'd not experienced it yet, yet he could well imagine. It was what happened to those who went against the pack.

Hell, he wasn't sure if he trusted himself. He deserved any condemnation they'd heap on his head, but knowing his best buds, they'd take offense and fight those who sought to punish Marc for his actions. He'd already fucked them over enough. Let them start their new life with their mate, Thea, free of friction. It was the best apology he could think of.

With that in mind, he remained a silent watcher, staying downwind of searchers, rolling in a patch of yarrow, the sweet scent of its crushed flowers a further ploy to mask his scent. However, no matter how close they came to discovering him, he didn't run away. He couldn't until he made certain of one thing.

As the dawn crested, he was as close to the edge of the forest as he dared, gaze trained on the lump of meat that had once sought to control all Lycans. He barely blinked as Roderick's body shriveled under the bright glare of UV rays, caving in on itself until flesh turned to dust.

As if this were a signal, the milling groups of remaining Lycans departed, off to celebrate their hard-earned victory and to bask in a sleep finally free of nightmares. It occurred to Marc he should leave too. *I should look for shelter.* But for some reason, he didn't move. He couldn't. It was almost as if he was compelled to remain. With nothing better to do, he stayed.

He wasn't alone.

Nathan, the son of the late Roderick, and his mate also stood vigil for a while, making certain, like

Marc, that the horror would never rise again. Eventually he, too, left, and Marc was alone with only regret for company.

The sun completed its journey across the sky and sank into the horizon, painting the asphalt in a brilliant wave of colors before giving way to twilight. Despite the insistent grumble in his belly, Marc kept his sentinel post.

Wind stirred the heavy ash pile on the ground, swirling it and yet not managing to disperse it. Much like metal filings when attracted to a magnet, the particles spun and danced but never strayed too far from their origin. Even the ashes from the decapitated head in the end managed to make their way back to the rest. Uncanny.

The parking lot gaped vacantly with only a few vehicles remaining to mark the sparse occupants staying at the hotel, most of them oblivious to the life-and-death battle that had raged. And, of those who remained, none were watching.

From the shadows trotted Marc, still in the form of his red-coated wolf, the bullet wound in his side clotted over but a reminder and punishment of what he'd done. Unable to help himself, he paused in front of a pockmarked hotel door, number seven, where the stench of bleach had wiped the blood away, a blood he'd drawn while under the control of another.

Not my fault. He knew that, and yet, he doubted he would ever manage to erase the memory of the act or the shame.

Backing away, his wolf whining, he sidled over to the pile of dust.

Of the monster, nothing tangible survived, not even his clothes. The hotness of Roderick's destruction had melted everything. Only dark ash, cooling now as night fell, remained. It emitted a charred odor of meat cooked too long.

The acrid scent intrigued his beast, who urged him to sniff. Despite suspecting it was a bad idea, he still lowered his nose. He inhaled, a tad too deeply, and immediately sneezed and then drew in a deep breath, accidentally sucking in a lungful of the stuff.

Ack. Gross. He coughed, hacking and sneezing right into the larger pile, which didn't help matters. Particles of ash lifted and formed a gray cloud, blinding him momentarily, clogging his throat and nasal passages.

Shaking his head, he sought to clear his senses, but while the dust drifted away, drawn back to the pile, he couldn't shake loose the foreboding sense he'd done something monumentally stupid. And gross. *I just snorted a dead werewolf vampire.* Hopefully it wouldn't act like cocaine and render him crazier than he already was.

Alas, a drug-induced haze didn't ensue, nor did he suddenly start seeing butterflies or rainbows. He did have an urge to sneeze again, though, but he held it in as someone approached.

Ears pricked, he heard the distinctive purr of an engine and rubber tires crunching on asphalt as it neared. Acute hearing was both a blessing and a curse for Lycans, although more of a curse when young and he couldn't help hear, even through the walls, his parents doing things no pup wants to think of. So much for his theory he'd been conceived via immaculate conception.

However, thinking of his traumatization as a boy wouldn't hide him from whoever drew near. He darted back to the shadowy edge of the woods, a protective barrier, where, once again, he turned to living stone and watched.

A dark sedan rolled into the parking lot, its lights extinguished, making it instantly suspicious. He could tell it was a luxury vehicle, despite its lack of identifying marks, by the subtle muted purr of its engine.

It stopped alongside the ash, and the rear passenger door opened, but no one exited. Instead, hands clad in black leather gloves emerged, bearing a small broom and dustpan. A few brisk strokes was all it took to sweep the dusty remains and deposit them in a carved wooden box, which made its appearance on the ground alongside the body.

What the hell? Marc couldn't fathom what the person was doing or why; however, he did suspect the who. The scent…He knew that scent, and it sent a terrified shiver through him.

Vampire. The knowledge froze him, and while his wolf urged him to flee, he feared even the slightest motion, or noise, would bring the attention of the creature on him. He didn't want to be caught. *I can't be a mindless slave again.* He'd rather die first.

But death wasn't in the cards, not for him, not today.

When all the ash had been moved from the pavement to the receptacle, the mysterious gloved hands withdrew. The car door closed, and the vehicle drove away with none to mark its passage. It disappeared into the shadows from whence it arrived with only a russet wolf, a traitor to his kind, as witness.

Why does a vampire want the ashes? He wasn't sure he wanted to find out.

Chapter Three

One moment, the oppressive pressure constantly pushing at the barrier of Antonia's mind was there, doing its best to creep in, and the next it was gone.

Vanished. Extinguished like the candle given to her days ago. But while the candle left a sign of its existence in the form of a glob of wax on the dirty stone floor, the overbearing presence that she'd grown used to in her head evaporated without a trace.

Only once it disappeared did she realize just how much it had weighed on her. Stifled her. Tainted her with its vile and dark oily feel. How light she suddenly felt. She even managed a smile, the first in what seemed like forever. *I'm free. Free of that bastard.*

Not entirely, or so she reminded herself considering her current location.

Her momentary elation couldn't last when faced with reality. Mentally free didn't equal physically free, but then again, judging by the noise coming from outside her cell, that was perhaps a good thing.

What's happening? Something big, of that she was certain. Had the evil one who'd captured her finally died? Was that why she no longer felt him trying to force her to his bidding? Were his torturous visits finally at an end? Judging by the frenzied yelling, the dark leader of the bastards who'd kidnapped her was not coming back. And those left behind didn't handle it well.

The howling of wolves, lots of them, went on for hours while the screaming of humans lasted mere moments. Fragile flesh couldn't stand for long before claws and teeth. She knew that firsthand. Her captor had delighted in making her watch those short matches.

Man versus wolf. But not just a wolf, a werewolf, creatures of myth and nightmares, real, all too real and savage.

She still shuddered at the recollection of her first experience with one, the day of her kidnapping, a day she preferred to forget.

The knock on her door saw her scrambling for the cash she'd pulled out of her wallet. Friday night pizza. Alone, but not unhappy about it given she had DVR'd the latest episode of Sleepy Hollow. *She flung open the door, expecting to see her usual delivery guy, with his baseball cap askew, his smile wide and displaying an impressive array of braces.*

Instead, a pair of unshaven gents pushed their way in, each cinching one of her arms in a meaty hand to drag her back. She opened her mouth to scream, only to have a balled piece of fabric stuffed into it.

What the hell?

Home invasion? Did these thugs not realize she didn't own anything worth stealing?

So intent was she on spitting out the gag and struggling to break free that she didn't notice the third man who walked in. However, once the door slammed shut behind him, and the chill of his presence arrowed its way through her panic, she stilled. Fear, unlike anything she'd ever experienced, made her tremble. The terror invaded every portion of her being, a dread worse than when she'd bungee jumped the first time, a trepidation greater than when she'd paced in the hospital waiting room as her father underwent bypass surgery.

She looked upon the face of true evil and silently apologized to her mother when she'd scoffed at the existence of demons. Hard to mock when a demon stood before her, not that he bore the appearance of one.

On the surface he seemed human, with once dark hair peppered with gray, the ends uneven as if hacked off with no care for style. His sallow skin, stretched taut, sported a five o'clock shadow. A beakish nose, red veined and prominent, offset his jowly cheeks. Perhaps once a handsome man in his youth, but age and unhealthy living had done a number on him. But that wasn't what brought the chill to her spirit. One had to only look into his eyes and read the sadistic sneer on his bloodless lips to know something was deeply wrong with this man.

His eyes bored into hers, an unblinking stare that she couldn't look away from. The longer she gazed into his eyes, the more sure she became that the pinpricks of red in his irises weren't a trick of light or her imagination. The red flare grew, as did the mocking leer.

"Hello, Antonia." The low treble of voice sent ghostly spiders skittering across her skin. She shivered.

How does he know my name?

"I'm sure you're wondering why I'm here. I'd tell you, but then you'd have nothing to look forward to. I find anticipation seasoned with a dose of dread and despair so much more delicious. But I'm not completely cruel. I will give you one

hint. It's going to hurt. Hurt a lot."

The callous announcement broke the spell, but her fight to escape ended before it began. She was no match for the men, and thus did her punishment begin. But no one could call Roderick a liar.

He was right. It hurt.

Remembering the past wasn't something Antonia liked indulging in, and it wasn't hard to find distraction from those less than cheerful memories with the destruction being wrought outside her cell. The eerie howls and snarls were nonstop and frightening because for every ululation there was a yelp, an inhuman scream of an animal injured.

Another wolf bites the dust.

What that would mean for her, she didn't even want to think of. Was this the day the cavalry came to the rescue? Was the battle for her freedom being fought? Or would she exchange one horrific existence for another with a new master at the helm?

Huddled in a corner, she could only hug her knees and pray as the frantic sounds of battle and mayhem permeated the air of her prison. Objects, bodies she suspected given what she heard, slammed against the locked door of her cell, and for once she didn't curse the thickness of the barrier, not when it was the only thing she suspected kept her safe.

All through the night, insanity reigned. By the next dawn, or so she gauged by the sunlight that managed to creep its way through the bars over her window, the chaos, or the noise of it at any rate, subsided until only a chilling silence remained. Once she would have welcomed the quiet, but now, instead, she feared. What did it mean? The silence became even more ominous as time passed and her belly rumbled.

What had happened to her jailers? *Did they all leave?* On the one hand, she silently cheered. Antonia never wanted to deal with those sadistic bastards again or have to pity the cowering ones with their minds caught by the evil one.

But on the other hand, if all who remembered her existence had died or left, then who would set her free? *No one knows I'm here.*

Panicked, she scrambled to her feet and crossed the few steps to pound on the door. She screamed and kicked the thick portal. She hit it until her hands were bleeding and bruised. She hollered until her voice emerged as a hoarse croak. No one answered her call. She slumped to the stone floor and sobbed.

One day stretched into two then three by her count. With only the water from the rusted sink to sustain her, she grew weak. Antonia also couldn't help but face the ugly truth.

I'm going to die here, just not in the way she'd initially assumed. Before, she'd imagined her evil captor or his minions killing her. Now? Now the joy she'd thought she'd feel at never seeing them again paled as the horror of dying by starvation hit her.

No. I can't die this way. Not without a fight or a chance. But what could she do? She was locked in a room with no way to escape. The door wouldn't budge; on the contrary, its solid nature mocked her.

The real tease, though, was the breath of air and light that managed to creep in through the only other opening.

For the millionth time since her incarceration, Antonia clung to the bars that covered the tiny window set in the rear wall. The glass was long gone, and weeds provided a curtain across the opening. Antonia had tried to eat those at one time, but their bitterness soon had her retching miserably. She'd find no sustenance in them.

With her fingers gripped tight around the firmly cemented rods, Antonia screamed until she was hoarse. "Someone. Help me. Please!"

No one answered her cry.

But she kept trying.

For hours she called, delirious with hunger, her body weakening. *Oh, say it like it is, you're dying.*

NO!

Except, the no was less a word and more a feeling, a feeling that wasn't hers alone.

A presence pulsed in her head, a wild thing that howled. A primal entity who wouldn't give up. Where she lacked the strength, it found some but, in so doing, pushed at the walls she'd erected to protect herself. The presence inside her gathered its strength, or did she relinquish control? Did it matter? She'd lost all hope.

And whatever lurked inside Antonia's head took advantage of her weakness of spirit. As her mind shattered, finally defeated, she forgot who she was. But she still retained enough wits to know freedom lurked just past the wooden portal. She could smell it. Craved it. Pined for it. Just like she could scent liberty from the opening in the wall, the one too small for her to squeeze through.

On stumbling feet, she made her way to the window. She craned her head and whimpered. So close…

Unable to stand the stench of her cell any longer, Antonia spent the rest of the day doing her best to inhale the fresher air wafting through the window. A death grip on the bars helped her to sleep standing up, her forehead resting on the wall, not caring that the rough cinderblocks scraped her skin. She dozed, dreaming of days when the worst that could happen was a car splashing through a puddle and soaking her as she walked to work.

The tingle in her fingers woke her, like hundreds of teensy, tiny pinpricks. Not painful, but not exactly pleasant either. Had the end come? Was her body preparing to shut down and send her to the ever after?

She peered at her fingers still wrapped around the rusted rods, the skin bathed in a sprinkle of moonlight. The odd sensation continued. Her skin prickled then burned, and before her horrified gaze, hair sprouted on the back on her hands. Thick, lush, dark hair.

Her mind babbled, *Oh my God. This can't be happening.* While she could only watch in disbelief, the presence now driving her body pulsed in excitement. It practically laughed with joy even, as the uncomfortable stinging turned into stabbing needles.

An agonized scream made its way out past her abused vocal cords. Pain. *Holy fucking hell, the pain.* Antonia dropped to her knees with a jolt, but that simple bruise was nothing compared to the agony lighting every nerve in her body. She toppled over and hit the floor on her side, body thrashing. Awareness retreated as she hid in the little room she'd built for herself in her mind for when Roderick visited. She hid in her safe spot and left her dying body alone. Well, not entirely alone. The entity in her mind exulted in the pain and changes. It encouraged her to remain hidden. So she did.

When the door to the cell opened, she never even noticed, but the wolf now dominating her body did, and it lunged for freedom.

Chapter Four

Marc couldn't have said what led him to the farmhouse in the middle of nowhere. He'd never seen the place before, and yet something had compelled him to come here. As he stared at the sagging porch, the peeling wooden boards paneling the exterior of the house, and the curled shingles on the roof, he couldn't help a sense of déjà vu.

Why does this place seem so familiar?

Why did he feel drawn to it? Actually he knew why. Signs of their presence and smell was everywhere. Rogues used to live here, but he doubted any did anymore. Not living ones at any rate, or so his wolf assured him. He'd yet to change back to his man form. Why would he? No clothes. No wallet. No reason. Best to stay as an animal for now. Maybe if he got lucky, a hunter would shoot him.

Although, he doubted it would happen here. Death had already visited and taken its due.

A few bodies littered the property, some of the mangled corpses partially hidden in the tall grass heavily speckled with weeds. The front porch sagged with the weight of a cadaver bent over its splintered railing. The scent and signs of a savage battle were plain to see everywhere he looked. The interior of the house wasn't spared. Rust-colored stains and blood long dried smeared the peeling white paint of the front door, a door left ajar.

Despite an urge to walk away, he forced himself over the threshold, leaving the waning warmth of the sun for the cool, tomb-like atmosphere within.

More of the documented violence awaited. Bloody handprints covered the faded roses on the buckling wallpaper. A puddle of it filled a dip in the floor, which he skirted around. No matter where he looked, or how shallowly he breathed, the odors of wolf, death, and vampire permeated everything.

I've found one of Roderick's lairs. It seemed, even with the bastard's death, Marc couldn't escape him.

Fuck me, what am I doing here? Just knowing he breathed the same air as the monster had made him want to run far and fast, but he didn't.

The same thing that drew him here wouldn't let him leave. Inside his head, his wolf whined. It didn't like this place. It wanted back outside where there was fresh air and the full moon beckoned. His four furry paws itched to run and bask in the cleansing beams. He resisted the urge.

I must do something. Find something. But what?

His twitching nose caught a vague scent, something that didn't belong amongst the chaos and evil he saw and scented everywhere he turned.

Closing his eyes, he inhaled deeper than he wanted, almost choking on the fetid aromas. It came to him again, the perfume of something…good? How could anything good have survived this mess? How could there be any good left anywhere?

He didn't have an answer, but he needed to find out.

With ginger steps, his paws dodged the nastier stains soaking into the wood floors that had long ago lost their varnish. He trotted from the hall into a kitchen, or he should say more like a nursery for flies and maggots. Rotted food, dirty dishes, and empty food cartons lay strewn everywhere, and the buzz of flies formed a constant hum that took only moments to set his teeth on edge. He'd salvage nothing here. What he sensed didn't hide in the kitchen. It was past a door beside the fridge down a flight of steps.

The basement had not escaped the violence, nor had the humans kept prisoner here survived. Thank goodness for his wolf and his lack of a gag reflex. Upon seeing the savagery, Marc felt sure he would have tossed the contents of his stomach.

The poor humans, captives he'd judge by the chains and shackles binding them to the wall. Manacled as they were, they hadn't stood a chance. When Roderick died, so did his control over his rogues, and while Marc welcomed the freedom, it seemed it drove others to madness.

And evil.

Gnawed limbs, bodies ripped apart, everywhere he looked evidence of unspeakable horrors mounted, enough that he wanted to flee. *And we will*, his wolf assured him. They just needed to do one thing first.

But what? *What task is so important that I must stay*

a moment longer in this cesspool of death and evil?

His wolf didn't answer, and his intuition also remained silent. The space didn't have anything of interest, if one ignored the bodies. Stripped of everything and made into a veritable dungeon, there was no furniture, no boxes, nothing. Nothing except one wooden door with a thick fucking padlock.

And of course, that was the door he needed to open.

Whining, his beast paced in front of the portal while Marc pondered the situation.

What's hiding behind the door? One of Roderick's psychos waiting to rip his throat out? More bodies in various states of decay? Another vampire?

It took only one sniff to assure him that the good thing he sensed awaited.

Shifting to his man shape took effort, especially with the full moon begging his Lycan genes to join the lunar goddess in a wild dance through the woods. God, how he wanted to run and forget and cleanse himself of the evil that surely coated his skin.

Yet, despite his trepidation, he had to open the door. It didn't even matter why or what was behind it. He just knew it was imperative, which meant he needed to either find bolt cutters or a key.

With a heavy sigh, he turned around and perused the abattoir. *Want to bet one of the bodies had it?* Lucky him, he'd get to go corpse robbing.

Cringing and gagging, he wondered what *Fear Factor* would think if he suggested searching dead mangled bodies as a stunt.

Ridiculous thoughts like these kept his mind from delving too deep into his action. Finally, chance was on his side, and he located a key ring clipped to a belt with an O-ring on the third body he searched.

Ignoring the shiver of his naked frame, which protested the dank dampness of the cellar, he inserted the key into the lock. New and still well oiled, it popped open with barely a *click*. Tearing it off the clasp, he allowed himself only one deep breath before pulling at the handle and opening it.

Nothing could have prepared him for the petite female wolf that came barreling out. Without pause, the dark-haired creature, her eyes wide with fear and madness, bolted past him, up the stairs, and, he'd wager, out the door.

What? No thank you?

It seemed he'd just rescued one of Roderick's victims. Or had he doomed her to a different kind of death? The way she'd fled, the scent of terror clinging to her fur and leaving a tangible trail, she was a beacon to any predators who fed on weakness.

I should go after her. And do what? Protect her? He'd been unable to protect himself and his friends when it mattered. What made him think he'd do her any good?

I have to try. Perhaps he wasn't ideal hero material, but at the moment, he was all she had. And some protection was better than nothing. But first, he needed to do one thing.

It wasn't hard to find a lighter nestled inside a

pack of cigarettes. It was even easier to light the cardboard pizza boxes in the kitchen, the orange flicker of the flame hungrily devouring the dry fuel.

Only once the fire danced high enough to not get extinguished by a puff of air did Marc allow himself to exit the house of horrors.

As he switched back into his wolf shape, the acrid scent of smoke began to billow from the open door, but he didn't stay to watch the abattoir burn. Instead, he followed the trail of a wolf.

Chapter Five

During his escape from the castle, where his council of peers tried to murder him, Thaddeus had to kill two thralls and one vampire, whose head he lobbed from a window, and maimed two vampires—the arm he tore off would eventually grow back, but not the earlobe he bit and swallowed.

Did he fight dirty? Damned straight. One didn't live to a ripe old age by showing courtesy to the enemy. *If you're going to attack me, you'd better come prepared.* A lesson they'd never learned, and so they failed. Losers. As coups went, Morpheus didn't plan very well, and he'd underestimated Thaddeus's strength.

Did this mean it was over? That Thaddeus was scot-free? Of course not. Morpheus would try again, of that Thaddeus was certain, which meant returning to his home was a bad idea.

A shame, Thaddeus had grown quite fond of the penthouse condo he'd bought in the city. Perhaps once he'd prevailed over his enemies, he'd return. Or buy a new one. When one was immortal, it was always best to never stay in one place for too long.

With his home out of the question, what to do?

Self-preservation said he should hide. Over the years, Thaddeus had acquired a stable of residences around the world, places he could run to when in need of solitude or a change. However, he chose not to.

For one thing, he couldn't be sure a welcoming committee, one better prepared, wouldn't await him. Secondly, ducking for cover wouldn't warn the wolves or other vampires of the nefarious plot to bring their existence to light and start a war.

And thirdly? Thaddeus didn't fucking want to. Call it pride or foolhardiness, but either way, he wasn't in the mood to bow down to a power-crazy asshole who couldn't find his own dick in the dark without help—a taunt he'd shouted at Morpheus as he fled the council chambers and the ambush.

With remarks like that, Thaddeus didn't have to wonder why he didn't have many friends.

Insults aside, he needed a plan. Thaddeus hadn't made it to a ripe age making foolish decisions. How Morpheus had survived was anyone's guess, but Thaddeus would have called it stupid, blind luck, a luck that was about to end if he kept up with his insane plan to start a war.

Such foolishness. Especially now with cameras built into every cell phone and the technology the government had at its fingertips.

Did Morpheus and his posse of sycophants not understand the suicidal aspect of their plan? If humanity were to discover them and wage a war of extinction, odds were humans would win.

Vampires might have been creatures to fear back in the days of swords and daggers and pitchforks—*ooh, look at me with my big scary eyes, sharp teeth, and superstrength!*—but in today's modern world of guns—because bullets to the brain didn't heal very well—and UV lights, vampires would not fare well. Not well at all.

Extinction was a very real possibility because, contrary to popular belief, vampires couldn't just replicate without consequence.

On the contrary, only the strongest created progeny because for every vampire they created they had to give up some of their own power. It was why Thaddeus chose to remain a master with few minions. Call it greedy, but Thaddeus wasn't about to share his strength with anyone else. Which was probably why Morpheus would spare no expense or effort in trying to bring him down. *Like fuck is he going to cannibalize my ass.*

So, with his homes off-limits, unsure of whom he could trust in the vampire world, and not quite willing to throw himself at the mercy of wolves, what options did he have?

Thaddeus needed allies. But despite his boast to the council, he wasn't sure who of his own kind he could trust. Given Thaddeus didn't play well with others, he was considered somewhat of a recluse—and a bastard. His reputation for ruthlessness preceded him, even if he'd given up killing for no reason a few decades ago. That his kind deserved warning went without saying, but they weren't the ones in immediate danger.

I need to warn the dogs. Sounded easy on the surface, but he doubted it. While he'd spoken to

Nathan, pack alpha, once before, he hadn't been too sure how his words would be received. For all he knew, the wolves would welcome a chance for vengeance given what Roderick had done. Perhaps the wolves would encourage a war and a chance to wipe out vampires so that never again would one of their own become an almost unstoppable monster.

Only one way to find out. But not here. Not so close to the council and Morpheus's troops.

Thaddeus fled on foot, his speed not quite that of a car but quick enough to distance him from those hunting him. Only once he found himself perched on the rooftop of a posh hotel, where he'd registered as a guest, paying cash for his room, did he whip out his cell phone and scroll through its numbers.

As he listened to it ring, he only vaguely noted the time, four a.m. Hmm, perhaps not a great time to wake someone up. He shrugged. It couldn't be helped.

A groggy voice answered, "This better be fucking important."

"Did the doggy's nap get interrupted?" Thaddeus couldn't help his sarcasm. Centuries of living gave him a sense of superiority that was hard to overcome.

"You." One word, spoken with disgust.

"Yes, me. My, but don't we seem overjoyed."

"What did you expect? You fucking hung us out to dry when Roderick slipped your grasp." It seemed Nathan bore a grudge. Too fucking bad.

"And yet, you prevailed." To the surprise of many. Even Thaddeus, who had been in the midst of preparing himself for battle, had been impressed when the news arrived that Roderick was no more.

"We took down the fucker, no thanks to you."

"Excuse me, dog? Have you so soon forgotten the knowledge I gave you to aid you in vanquishing your foe?"

"Actual help would have been better. But no, instead you and your other bloodsucking buddies hid like fucking cowards while we cleaned up your mess."

Funny how Nathan echoed his words to the council. "Does this mean you're going to try and welch out of the favor you owe me?"

"As far as I'm concerned, you owe me. We stopped Roderick, and not without casualty. But the nightmare isn't over. Now I've got a bunch of victims, some of them stark-raving mad, to deal with. Whatever mind tricks your kind can play have left them a menace to society."

"I might be able to help."

"The same way you helped before?" Nathan snorted. "No thanks."

"I did not call to engage in an argument over who is to blame. There are grave matters afoot."

"Let me guess, these matters somehow involve my pack?"

How Thaddeus enjoyed the directness of those with short life spans. They cut to the heart of the matter without the endless crap. "It involves not just your pack but all the wolves. Even humanity."

"Of course it does." A heavy sigh came through the phone speaker. "I'd like to tell you to fuck off with your melodrama, but on the off chance you have something important to say that does impact my pack, I guess I need to listen."

"Smart move, dog."

A rumble came through the earpiece. "I dare you to say that to my face, blood sucker."

"I just might. I dare say we'd have fun. However, I didn't call to insult but to warn. It has recently come to my attention that there are those of my kind who think that you and your pack, as well as any of Roderick's survivors, require elimination."

"Elimination as in killing? Why?" Nathan's bafflement came through quite clearly.

"Because you are aware of our existence."

A pregnant silence followed. Thaddeus waited.

"Uh, I hate to break it to you, but everyone knows about vampires. Or have you not been to a movie theater lately or a bookstore?"

A grin stretched Thaddeus's lips. Nathan did not fear him. It was refreshing to say the least. "Ah yes, the *Twilights* and *True Bloods* and other modern-day romanticisms of vampire and wolf. People are aware of fictional vampires. They have been for centuries, but they don't truly believe. On the other hand, your pack is aware that we are real, as are the rogues."

"And?"

"And the council that governs all vampires fears you will tell others."

Nathan laughed. "Tell who exactly? The *New York Times*? Has all that blood drinking addled your brains?"

"That was my reply to their absurd claim. However, they are quite emphatic that you need to be culled."

"Over my dead fucking ass," Nathan growled.

"They assumed that would be your reply. As a matter of fact, they were hoping for it."

It didn't take long for Nathan to grasp the implication. "Hold on a second. You mean they want us to fight? But why?"

"Boredom. Power. I'm sure I could come up with a list of reasons if you really wanted more than one."

"But they risk exposing us all if they do that because we're hardly going to bare our throats and die quietly."

"It's what they're hoping for. It seems they don't fear exposure. They want to come out of the closet, so to speak. And they intend to drag the Lycans along with them."

"They're fucking nuts." The spaced-out words were rife with incredulity.

"Yes."

"You're fucking serious about this?"

"Very. Do I seem like a man who calls pack alphas to make absurd claims?"

"I don't know what you like to do for shits and giggles."

"Dangle worthless criminals from rooftops until

they cry for their mothers." Thaddeus also enjoyed walks in the park, looking for muggers and rapists to chase. And visiting prisons to spook the inmates into renouncing their wicked ways. Oh, and the debauching of virgins, especially those born to religious families.

Apparently, his flippant remark threw Nathan for a loop. "Excuse me? What the fuck does dangling criminals have to do with your crazy-ass buddies?"

"How I entertain myself is of no importance. We need to act before the council does."

"Yeah, I get that, but one thing I don't understand is why you're telling me this. Shouldn't you be siding with your friends?"

"One, they are not my friends. Friends require maintenance and favors. They also expect you to keep your hands off their girlfriends. I prefer solitude."

"So you're doing this to spite them?"

"In a sense. Suffice it to say, not all of us agree to this suicidal plan."

"Obviously you're one of them. How many others are on your side?"

"For now, none, but I am sure once I speak to others of my kind that I can muster a sufficient force to combat those who would destroy us all."

"You mean you've got nobody to back you?" Nathan sputtered.

"For now. But, I assure you that, even were I alone, I am a more than worthy opponent."

"Great, just fucking great. An offer of help from the one fucking vampire no one likes or trusts," Nathan muttered.

"It's better than nothing."

"We'll see about that. So what do you want me to do? How can I keep my people safe?"

"Keep them close. Do not leave the compound at night. While my kind have the power of persuasion, it is usually ineffective against Lycans."

"Roderick didn't seem to have a problem," Nathan reminded him.

"Ah, but Roderick was once Lycan. We believe that played a factor in his ability to manipulate."

"So there're no other wolf-vampire hybrids we need to worry about?"

"No."

"So why the warning, then? If you can't mojo us, then why the precautions?"

"Because there is a possibility that those who've been influenced before might prove susceptible."

"Fucking rogues. I should have gone with my first instinct and killed them all," Nathan grumbled.

Despite the low tone, Thaddeus heard a female murmur saying, "You're not a killer. We'll figure out something."

"Do you have many in your care?" Thaddeus queried.

"Some. Not all. By my count, there's probably dozens of others roaming the state. Or not. Once Roderick died, most of them went crazy. We've got some on suicide watch. Others, we're keeping under lock and key because they turned violent and seem intent on challenging and fighting. Given the behavior of the ones we captured, I can't see the ones on the loose faring much better. Chances are most will die by their own hand or doing something stupid."

"That's too much to leave to chance. These rogues, as you call them, are currently roaming without rules or a leader, which makes them vulnerable to my kind, which, in turn, makes all the packs vulnerable."

"How?"

"If another vampire were to find one of these minions and acquire them for his own, he could use that wolf to gain entry into your pack or another."

Nathan caught on quick to his train of thought. "Trojan horse."

"Exactly. Wreak havoc and sabotage from within. It is imperative we gather these wandering wolves and contain them."

"Easier said than done. We've been looking for them. Wherever they've run off to, they're not coming back. And with what you've just told me, I can't afford to send my men haring off, making them susceptible for capture, and leaving the pack without a firm line of defense."

A valid point, and one Thaddeus doubted he could budge Nathan from. "What if I found them for you?" Why he made the offer, Thaddeus couldn't have said. He wasn't a bloodhound to go sniffing and hunting after wolves. However, if he wished to ally himself with Nathan, and prevent his brethren from implementing their plan, then he needed to do everything he could to keep the mentally injured Lycans at large from falling into Morpheus's hands.

"How are you going to locate them?"

"I have a way."

A way he'd hoped to avoid.

Chapter Six

The newly born wolf ran. And ran. And ran some more her first night of freedom. The fresh air, crisp and clean, burned her lungs as she exerted herself, but it burned in a good way. A free way.

It felt so good to have escaped. To bathe in the light of the moon. To lap at the cold water of the stream and chase down the squirrel for sport and much-needed food.

As to the annoying buzz in her head that pounded and cried, the wolf ignored her. The weak one wasn't in charge anymore. *She* was. And she had no intention of relinquishing control anytime soon.

She wouldn't be imprisoned again.

It wasn't until the dawn that she slowed her mad dash, her limbs finally tiring. A rocky outcropping provided an alcove for shelter where none could sneak up on her. She curled into a ball, muzzle tucked onto her forelegs, and closed her eyes, trusting in her hearing and senses to alert her if danger approached.

How long she slept she couldn't gauge, but it wasn't enough to feel fully rested. The sun had not even crested the midpoint in the sky, and yet something woke her. A noise. A scent. Something intruding on her space.

Raising her head, she sniffed, allowing the

various odors to filter, and she pricked her ears to listen.

What was making the fur on her back rise?

There it was. Faint, barely noticeable. A shift in the light breeze brought it to her. A musky animal odor, that of another wolf, a male.

With keen eyes, she perused the area before her, searching for the intruder. She didn't spot him at first; his russet coat blended well with the autumn foliage and its myriad colors in shades of red and orange. A tremble of leaves gave him away.

Her lip peeled back in a snarl, and her chest vibrated as she rumbled a warning. *Stay away.*

He didn't heed her warning and stepped out of concealment and approached, slowly. He didn't cower, he didn't attempt to assert dominance, but he wasn't going away. His gaze locked with hers as he took careful, measured steps. She rose to stand on all four of her paws, hackles raised, her growl intensifying. Even though she didn't sense danger from the stranger, she wasn't about to show weakness. She'd not escaped one set of males to allow another to dominate her.

Far enough to give himself time to move but close enough she could scent him—his odor not unpleasing, rather intriguing—the male lay down and pillowed his head on his paws. She waited for him to speak a challenge. Or lunge. Do something.

He closed his eyes.

It confused her, especially since she knew he didn't sleep. Despite her tugging fatigue, neither did she. Gaze trained on him, she watched him, relaxing after a time when he didn't make any sudden moves. How long they might have stayed that way was debatable. However, her stomach grumbled—as did the *other* in her mind.

The one she ignored. She wasn't about to relinquish control yet, not when she'd just managed to emerge. The other grumble, the physical one, needed tending. Time to find food, but the russet wolf blocked her path. To go hunting she would have to pass him. Giving him her flank or back was not an option. She stood and paced before the alcove she'd rested in, a low whine rising unbidden from her throat. He lifted one lazy eyelid and regarded her.

She snarled.

He yawned wide, his large canines glinting in the waning afternoon sun. Coming to his feet, he gave himself a shake, the fur on his frame ruffling as he stretched. With a short yip, he bounded toward the forest but stopped at the edge. He craned to peer back at her and yipped again, this time inclining his head toward the shadows caused by the tree boughs.

He wishes us to hunt together.

A part of her didn't trust him, yet she also knew he wasn't one of those who'd hurt her before. She could tell by his scent. Oddly enough, she wanted to trust him. To hunt with him. To run. And perhaps indulge in wilder things…

With an answering bark, she bounded toward, then past, him. Time to find something yummy for dinner and then maybe some activity for dessert.

Chapter Seven

Marc's wolf shape didn't allow him to sigh, but he let one loose in his mind. When he'd first tracked down the female he'd freed, she'd reacted with distrust. He couldn't blame her. Having seen the state of the house, knowing what Roderick was capable of, he could only imagine her incarceration at the vampire's hands had proved less than pleasant.

When he came across her, huddled under a rock outcropping, her lip peeled back in a snarl, it occurred to him for a moment to shift into his human shape and try reasoning with her. Not a great idea, especially if it set her off and she decided to attack him in his more vulnerable form. With manbits to protect, he stuck to his wolf and settled down to wait. And wait.

The female seemed determined to outlast him. He fought not to twitch or grumble or drool because she emitted the most pleasing scent. He wondered if he'd have to give in and perhaps come back later after he sated some pressing needs, but his waiting finally paid off. Hunger stirred her. He heard the grumble of her stomach, and when she stood to pace, distrust still evident, he gave her some space and then invited her to hunt with him.

To Marc's surprise and delight, she agreed,

bounding off with him into the woods to track down some slow critters for a repast. It became quickly evident that, whoever the female was, she'd not been a wolf long or at least had never belonged to a pack. While her instinct when it came to prey was good, her technique was clumsy. Her finesse in eating messy and the occasional horrified glint in her eyes a dead giveaway that the woman inside was not used to such savagery—or wild delicacies.

Only once they'd finished their meal and found a cool stream to drink from, and wash the blood from their muzzles and paws, did he decide it was time.

Shifting shapes was never pleasant, no matter how many times he did it. It became especially challenging when attempting to keep the urge to scream in pain stifled. He didn't want to do anything to frighten her off.

Lucky for him, the female watched the process, ears pricked and eyes wide. Kneeling on the spongy ground, naked and freckled, Marc tossed her a wan smile.

"Would you believe me if I said it's worse than it looks?"

She chuffed but didn't flee.

"Ready to give it a try?"

A violent shake of her head and a step back had him holding up his hands in a conciliatory gesture.

"Easy. Don't run off. I know it looks scary."

The female growled.

"I didn't mean to imply you were cowardly. But you will have to change back eventually."

Again, the she-wolf made a noise, and he was struck with a realization. "Or is that you don't want to change back? Or, more accurately, that your wolf won't let you?"

If a wolf could have smirked, she did.

Marc shook his head. "Bad girl. You can't just keep your other half imprisoned. It was her body first. You need to share."

The rumble and show of teeth didn't agree.

"Whoever is inside, listen to me, you don't have to let her control you. It's your body. Your choice. You can take back control whenever you want. You just have to want it. Take it. Don't let your inner bitch call the shots. I know you're tougher than that. You'd have to be. You survived Roderick."

He could almost see the struggle within her. The eyes flashed, one moment humanly aware, the next feral. A battle for control was waging in her mind, a war that saw skin rippling and caused snarls and even a sharp bark of discontent.

In the end, the woman who'd managed to stay alive in the dirty cell won. A mournful howl of loss—and annoyance at losing the mental battle—turned into a cry of pain, but the woman had guts because she clamped her lips tight and tried to muffle them.

Fur gave way to lightly tanned flesh, her Latina heritage evident in her exotic features and skin. Long strands of hair extended from her scalp to frame an exotic face and drape over bare shoulders, barely covering the rounded swell of heavy breasts.

He averted his gaze, less out of respect and more out of fear he'd embarrass himself. Or get called a pervert.

The woman possessed a shapely body. Only a dead man wouldn't notice—or react.

Once transformed back to her human self, she took a few heaving breaths before asking, "What the fuck happened to me?"

"I was kind of hoping you'd tell me. While I let you out of some basement prison, I don't know how you got there."

"I wasn't talking about my kidnapping, I mean, the whole furry fucking animal thing. I was a wolf!"

"Yes."

"A fucking wolf."

Someone has a potty mouth. He couldn't help the tilt of his lips as he shot her an amused glance. "I thought we'd already ascertained that."

Her scowl deepened. "That can't be, though. I'm human. A hundred percent human."

"Was."

"What do you mean was? I wasn't bitten by any of those fleabag assholes while imprisoned, so how the hell did I go from normal to four-legged bitch chasing goddamned squirrels?" Her voice rose in pitch as she let anger provide a cover for her fear.

"Roderick." One word, but it acted like a bomb of silence. And terror.

Funny, how a simple name could make them both shiver and, in her case, cause her to break out in sweat, terror an acrid odor exuded by her pores and plainly evident in her bearing. She sprang to her feet and cast a frightened look around. Any idiot with eyes in his head could tell she was close to fleeing.

He hastened to reassure her. "He's dead. You don't have to be scared anymore."

She regarded him, her mistrust in him, a stranger, warring with her need for reassurance. "Are you positive he's dead? Roderick is not normal. Not human."

"I am very sure. I watched his head fly off his shoulders and then had a front-row seat as he was burned by our good friend the sun. He's not coming back."

The relief had her slumping to the ground in a boneless heap. Her head dipped, and hair swung down to cover her face, but it couldn't quite mask the silent tears that shook her whole torso, nor could she hide their distinctive salty scent.

At a loss, Marc remained crouched, afraid to touch her and give her support, feeling like an asshole for his hesitation. *She's hurting. Why the fuck aren't I giving her a shoulder to cry on?*

Because, of all people, he shouldn't be anywhere near a Roderick victim, not given what he'd done. Yet, on the other hand, he was all this mystery woman had for the moment. Could he really just sit there and do nothing?

Only an asshole would let her cry without an attempt at comfort. And, while Marc was a lot of things, he did try not to be an asshole. He crab-walked over, slowly so she'd hear him coming, and when she didn't shy away, he tendered out an awkward hand to pat her on the back.

The soft silk of her skin branded him, and he almost scuttled away at the instant reaction—or more specifically the inappropriate reaction of his body. Before he could, she threw herself at him, locking her arms around his neck, pressing herself to him, sobbing noisily.

Good idea or not, he let his arms wrap around her, and he hugged her back, close to tears himself. He understood the relief at escaping Roderick's grip. He understood the horror he'd have to live with the rest of his life because of the vampire. Marc also understood that she was much too attractive and was having a distinct effect on his cock, a fact he tried to hide by shifting his legs to keep it from poking her.

They clung to each other for a while, survivors of a tragedy, until the sun sank well below the horizon. Only as the crickets began their nightly chirp, did she, with a sniffle, finally pull away.

"I don't suppose you've got a tissue," she jested in a watery voice.

He shook his head.

She sighed. "Figures. Then you might want to hum for a second because I am going to be totally gross and unladylike for a moment."

And then she did the most amazing thing, she farmer snorted in the bushes. Marc gaped. Then laughed. *I don't think I need to worry about her state of mind*. Anyone woman with balls like that was going to be just fine.

Chapter Eight

Antonia's cheeks burned bright. Talk about a fucked-up day. Life. Or was it a dream/nightmare? Given recent events, she really had to wonder about her grip on reality.

She'd gone from being a vampire's torture toy, to thinking she would die of starvation as a prisoner, to becoming some savage wolf, to hugging a naked stranger and blowing her nose in the bushes. What happened to going to work as a dental assistant, enjoying a beer after work, and watching *Sleepy Hollow*?

How long ago that normal life seemed. How she missed her comfortable apartment with its second-hand furniture and her fuzzy slippers. She especially wished for her flannel pajamas given how chilly it had gotten, now that night had fallen and she only wore…nothing.

"Fuck!" she couldn't help but exclaim when her nude state finally sank in. And lucky her, she wasn't just naked. She had an audience, a man just as naked as her, whom she'd hugged. Naked.

Her mother would have fainted and then had her doing a zillion Hail Marys if she'd been present. But her mother was far away in sunny Florida, enjoying her condo and the beaches with Antonia's father.

Thank God they'd not gotten involved in this

mess. However, thinking about them and her mother's reaction wouldn't clothe her or make the even hotter heat in her cheeks disappear.

She adopted a nonchalant stance because, hey, what was the big deal with hanging out in the woods bare assed with a cute, naked guy? "I take it no Kleenex means no clothes either." She dared a peek in his direction and was somewhat relieved to find him looking the other way but less so when she noted his hands very obviously trying to cover a hard-on, which, given her stance standing over him, he wasn't succeeding very well at. Not sure if she should be flattered or freaking, she looked away.

"Sorry, no clothes. It didn't even occur to me to grab some before I burned the house down."

"Burned the house? Do you mean the place they held me prisoner?" She turned back to glance at him in time to catch the nod of his head.

"Yeah, I did. Sorry. I couldn't just leave it there. Not with the smell of death and *him*." His lip curled at the last word.

Hearing his intense dislike of Roderick really helped ease the remaining trepidation in her. Anyone who hated that sadistic vampire was a friend in her book. "Don't apologize. I would have done the same if…" She trailed off as she recalled her mad-dash flight up the basement stairs and out the door as a four-legged beast.

He finished the sentence for her. "If you were yourself."

"That's one way of putting it." She sighed and

crossed her arms over her chest. Kind of late. He'd seen and probably felt most of her by now, and arms over her boobs did nothing for her kitty, which hadn't seen a razor in weeks. Still, it gave her a measure of comfort. "So what do we do now? Walk around like nudists on a nature hike until we come across help or a camper willing to loan us clothes?"

"Or we could swap back into our wolves."

A violent shake of head went well with her emphatic, "No!" As far as she was concerned, the furry monster who'd thrust her out of the way and possessed her body could stay locked up in her head.

"You don't need to fear your wolf."

"Says you. I wasn't exactly thrilled about being made a passenger in my own body, nor about what passed for dinner." Her stomach roiled in remembrance, but only the fear of vomiting fur and other nasty bits kept her from giving in to the temptation to purge.

"It only feels that way now. Over time, you'll find yourself in tune with your wolf. You'll understand her, and she'll learn to respect you. You won't have a choice. Your Lycan side has woken."

"Lycan side? What's that mean?"

"How about I explain as we walk? We should get moving if we plan to find shelter."

"You know, I was never really into the whole nature thing," she grumbled as she followed his lily-white ass into the canopy of trees. The brush and stones underfoot made her almost rethink her decision to stay human. Almost. She ignored the discomfort and caught up to her red-haired ally who strode ahead.

"Just because you're part wolf now doesn't mean you have to give up city living. You'll just need to make allowances for your other side a few times a month, especially around the full moon."

"You mean I'm going to go all werewolf every twenty eight days or so?"

"Probably. Or at least until you learn control, which isn't easy, especially for those without alpha tendencies."

"Whoa. Going too fast here. Control? Alphas? You mean all that made-up shit I watch on television is real?"

"To an extent. Television and movies tend to make it sound and seem more romantic and fun filled than the reality. Truth is we're just like everyone else."

"Used to be, you mean. Until you got bitten and turned into werewolves."

"Lesson number one, Lycans are born, not made."

"Um, hello, not born this way. I think my mother might have noticed she birthed a puppy. And while I need to shave my legs daily, I've never gotten any hairier, even on full moons."

He turned his head and smiled at her, and it was then she finally truly noticed him. Red ruffled hair, bright blue eyes, a freckled complexion, and an easygoing smile. He wasn't exactly what she'd consider classically good-looking, but she liked his face.

"What's your name?" she suddenly asked as it occurred to her that, while she more or less knew what he looked like naked, she hadn't the slightest clue who he was.

His grin widened. "I guess introductions are in order. Although, usually I know a girl's name before we get naked together for the first time."

It so closely mirrored her own thought, she couldn't help but laugh despite the situation. "I'm Antonia, but my friends and family call me Toni."

"Hello, Toni. I'm Marc, but my friends usually call me dumbass."

Again, she laughed. To her astonishment the sound was clear and not rusty, surprising given how long it had been since she'd had something to laugh about. "I would have said snow-white ass, but then again, I guess them knowing that depends on how close you are to them," she jested. It only occurred to her after that he might take offense. Her sense of humor was kind of raunchy, the joys of being raised in a family where male cousins outnumbered the female ones by almost four to one.

Marc chuckled. "Never fear. My delicate complexion, which can't stand much sun, has been the object of much amusement. The curse of being a redhead."

She moved the conversation back on track and away from his flexing ass cheeks. "So, Marc, when did you find out you were a wolf?"

"I always knew I was. Although, like others of

my kind, I didn't get to meet my furry side until I hit puberty. That's when most Lycans turn for the first time."

"Ouch. Changing voices, body odor, and a shaggy dog every full moon. That's what I call rough."

"Not really. Keep in mind, I grew up in a pack always knowing who I was and what I would become. For us, the first turning is a celebration."

"Most celebrations involve cake and balloons, not screaming pain."

"It gets easier."

Doubtful. "Yeah. Right. I saw your face. It hurt."

"It does. But you'll learn to accept and control the pain."

"We'll see about that. So this pack thing? What's it mean? Do all you wolf guys have some commune where you all live together and howl at the moon?"

He shook his head. "Yes and no. Yes, we kind of stick together, but other than that, we're just like regular folk. We live in houses. Go to work. Shop for groceries. Do everyday dumb shit. But when we're feeling frisky, or the moon is calling, we morph into wolves and run alone or together as a pack."

"Do you belong to a pack?"

"I used to." The smile on his lips faded.

"Why used to? What happened?"

"Same thing that happened to you, in a sense. Roderick came along and fucked my life up."

"But how? I mean you were already a wolf. What

did he do?"

"He made me do things. Bad things. To my friends. He made me hurt other wolves who had the strength to resist."

"And what, because you weren't yourself, your friends abandoned you?"

"No. But I couldn't exactly go back."

"Why not? I thought they were your friends."

"And because of me they almost died." He bit out the sentence with bitterness.

"But—"

"No buts." He stopped walking to turn a face twisted with anger—but also torn with anguish—her way. "I did some bad shit. I don't deserve their forgiveness. I don't want their fucking pity. I just want to be left the fuck alone."

"The same way you left me alone."

"That was different. You were scared and vulnerable, in danger if the wrong predator came along. I wanted to make sure you were all right."

"And you think your friends wouldn't forgive a guy who thinks nothing of chasing after some crazy broad in the woods without a thing to his name just to be a hero?"

He snorted with clear disdain. "I'm no hero."

"Whatever, superdog."

His eyes widened. "What did you call me?"

"Sorry, I guess the proper term would be superwolf. Saves bitches in distress, doesn't gag when faced with snot, and doesn't cop a feel or make sexual remarks in the face of a woman's nakedness. If those aren't the acts of a superwolf and hero, then I don't know what are."

A chuckle escaped him. "You're fucking whacked."

Another smile curved her lips. "Probably. I was a prisoner for a while. That's sure to mess with anyone's head."

"How long is a while?"

She rolled her shoulders. "You tell me. What's the date?"

"I don't know. I kind of lost track, too. October something or other."

"I was taken end of September. So over a month, at least. A month of being some vampire's screaming toy."

Marc winced. "Fuck. And I thought I had it bad. What did Roderick do to you? Did he and his lackeys, um, abuse you?" Marc ducked his head as he asked.

"Do you mean did they rape me? Then no. Grope me and threaten to? Yes. As for what Roderick did, I'm still not quite clear on that. He usually would come in taunting me with those freaky red eyes of his. Then, wham! Other than remembering pain. And screaming. Me screaming, that is, not much. I assume he did something to make me into a wolf." She shrugged. "I guess it's better if I don't remember what. I'd probably freak out if I did."

"From what little I know, Roderick found a way to make dormants active. And before you ask, a dormant is someone with the Lycan gene who doesn't manifest. In other words turn furry and howl. You're not the first woman he's tried to turn."

"You mean the sicko had more women prisoner? Where are they? Did you manage to save them, too?"

"You were the only person I found alive in that house. From what little I recall, he had a bunch of them all over the place. I guess he didn't want all his eggs or, in this case, his experiments and lackeys in one place."

A moue twisted her lips. "Experiment. How nice."

"Sorry."

"For what? It's not your fault. I guess I should count myself lucky in a sense. I survived."

"You did, and as soon as we reach civilization, I'll get you to the nearest pack where you'll be safe."

She halted again. "What do you mean get me to a pack? Once we get out of these woods, I'm heading for home and a hot shower. Thank God I gave my landlord postdated checks and had some money in the bank, or I'd be homeless."

"Going home might not be a good idea."

"Why not? Roderick's dead. You told me so yourself. I just want to forget this nightmare and go back to my life. My boring, no-vampire, no-werewolf life."

"Did you not hear what I said though about your Lycan side? You can't just pretend it doesn't exist."

Really? She intended to try. "If it's permanent as

you seem to think, then I'll go visit a national park on full moons and run around for a few hours." She started walking again, and after a moment, he caught up.

"It's more complicated than that. You can't ignore what you've become."

"No need to shove it in my face," she snapped. "I get that I won't be a normal girl anymore."

"There's more to it than that."

She halted and planted her hands on her hips. "More how?"

"There are rules. Laws. Lycan things you need to know so you can blend in and not give away our secrets."

"Trust me, I am not telling anybody about my ability to sprout fur and teeth. So don't worry, your secret is safe with me."

"That's not all. There are other things you need to know."

"Like what? Tips on keeping my wolf groomed? Getting flea baths twice a year? Using tomato juice if I get sprayed by a skunk? No eating my neighbor's noisy Pomeranian?"

The expression on his face flipped from amused, to outraged, to trying hard not to laugh, to determined. Hers went from didn't care to really didn't care.

"You're not taking this seriously," he said in a low tone.

"Did you really expect me to? Give me a break. Not so long ago, werewolves and vampires were fictional creatures. Now I'm one of them. I think I'm allowed a little slack."

"That attitude is why you need to stay with a pack for a while. They can teach you what it means to be Lycan. You might even find it more comforting in time to be surrounded by your own kind than humans. At least in a pack you don't have to hide who you are or have the neighbors look at you funny because you have more than one boyfriend."

She blinked. "Excuse me? More than one boyfriend?"

"Maybe even three or four."

"Are you calling me a slut?" Because, if he was, she had a foot ready to shove up his ass for the insult.

"No. Why would you say that?"

"I do not fuck multiple guys."

It was his turn to blink then grin at her sheepishly. "Oh. Yeah. I guess you not being pack and all you don't know. Lycan females are rare and birthrates low among our kind. As such, for generations now there's been a Pack law that states females must take on two with a max of up to four males as mates. You know, to improve the odds of conception and keep the gene pool fresh."

"But I'm not in a Pack, so your laws don't apply."

"You're wolf now. It's automatic. But don't worry. Nathan's been working to change them so the women now get to choose who they want to mate with instead of having random guys claim them."

Antonia, after all she'd gone through, had adapted fairly well. She'd had a momentary mental aberration. She still had a split personality with a wolf issue to deal with and a shivering body in need of clothes. But for some reason, his nonchalant declaration that she was expected to shack up with two or more guys—guys she could choose, how magnanimous—was the final straw.

She slugged him and, while he reeled, kneed him where it would really hurt.

Chapter Nine

Thaddeus returned to the place where Roderick had met his demise. He didn't have any problem finding it, especially given he'd volunteered to gather the remains when the death was confirmed, remains he'd managed to steal and bring with him when Morpheus betrayed him.

Morpheus probably had a hissy fit when he discovered the box in his possession was a decoy, filled with the useless ash of a campfire. As if Thaddeus would give the real, precious ash to that idiot. He wasn't stupid. Thaddeus knew his enemies would use it against him. Paranoia ever was his best friend.

After his unproductive phone call with the alpha leader, Thaddeus wasn't sure why he'd decided to revisit the parking lot. Despite his claim to Nathan he'd find the missing rogues, it wasn't as if Thaddeus expected to spot any of them milling around waiting for a collar, nor did he intend to put his nose to the ground in hot pursuit. However, where Roderick went to his final destination—probably an express elevator to hell—was a starting point.

If the idiot alpha of the nearby pack wouldn't heed his warning or gather up the remaining dogs, then it was up to Thaddeus to locate them and take care of them as he saw fit.

Minions or Renfields or thralls, whatever you wanted to call them, couldn't roam free when the death of their master released them from service. Not only were their broken minds, minds now bereft of the master who guided them, fragile and, in many cases, shattered beyond repair, they knew too much about the one they served. Knew too many vampire secrets.

It behooved all his kind to ensure these lost minions didn't fall into the wrong hands, blabbering about vampires and their secrets, secrets that most would discount as the ramblings of mad men and women. However, there was always a chance the wrong, or right, person might take heed. Scientists in their quest for fame and glory didn't always stick to morality when presented with the scientific find of the century.

Who wouldn't want a crack at vampire blood, genes, and DNA and the possibility of discovering the cure to aging? A solution to fix mortality? It had taken them years of culling, accidents, memory changes, and misdirection to hide the results of the labs at Area 52. Aliens, indeed. No one ever suspected what happened one state over. After the seeded rumors of Area 51, no one ever heard of the sister laboratory. The military made sure of that.

So while Thaddeus had told Nathan he'd gather the scattered wolves as a favor, in truth, he did himself and those of his kind a favor while, at the same time, foiling Morpheus and entertaining himself.

How long since he'd enjoyed a chase in the woods? Gone back to the basics and relied on his skills as a hunter? Too long.

First things first. He needed to prepare. He already wore the latest in athletic gear—no unwieldy capes or ruffles for him. He sported athletic pants and a form-fitting black Lycra shirt. The better to blend with shadows.

On his feet were laced Nikes, all the better to run in. Because pockets weren't exactly plentiful—and ruined the line of his suit—he tossed his wallet, phone, and keys inside the trunk for his car. But before he shut the lid, he leaned in to grab an ornate box. Less box and more a coffin for ashes. Roderick's ashes.

No matter how many times he did this over the years, the thought of what he had to do wasn't any more palatable. He flipped the lid and grimaced. The gray, ashy contents exuded a burned-pork-roast aroma. When human, he'd preferred beef.

Staring at it won't make it any easier. He sighed.

With both hands braced on the hood, Thaddeus lowered his face until it hovered over the dusty remains, and then he inhaled deep, sucked up the ash through both nostrils, appearing in that moment like an addict in need of cocaine or like one of those idiots on *Jackass* doing something monumentally stupid. In truth, he did what any other vampire would and had. He absorbed the essence of another to make himself stronger and hoped, in so doing, that he would be able to tune in to those Roderick once had ties to.

The greasy ash clogged his nasal passages. It gagged his throat. With a roar, he shook his head but didn't sneeze or cough. He couldn't, or this effort would go to waste. Bit by bit, his system absorbed the dust, and immediately he felt the difference. The strength, not much, not given the pinch he'd actually ingested, but enough for him to feel the rush. Which made the next snort, and the one after, easier and easier.

With each greasy inhalation and absorption, he felt his core essence grow stronger. His senses sharpened. His hunger thundered. His pulse, the electrical charge that animated him, unlike a corpse, which was a puppet, ticked faster. All of his sensory perceptions sharpened, became honed to a point he could sift various odors. Gas, rubber, asphalt, grass, wolf, wool…He almost went to his knees as the dozens of scents and their meaning hit him all at once.

Too much. Too many. Too…

Head bowed, he took to breathing shallowly through his mouth as his fingers pinched his nostrils shut. Kneeling on the pavement, it took him several moments to compose himself, to gain control over the tsunami of information battering its way through. He focused on the items, one at a time. The body he could handle, even if the rub of fabric on skin felt unnatural. *Fur is so much nicer.*

Where did that thought come from? He never wore fur. Fur was for women.

It seemed Roderick's spirit lingered strongly in his remains, unusual given he was ashed but not unheard of. Especially with the mentally strong ones.

I wonder if the drastic increase in my senses has to do with Roderick's Lycan heritage? What a dangerous secret if true, and knowledge that Thaddeus would keep to himself. The last thing they needed was power-hungry vampires trying to turn Lycans into vampires so that they could turn around and kill them to increase their own power base.

A logical explanation, for the overwhelming sensations helped battle them. Thaddeus released the hold on his nose and breathed, this time more prepared for the bombarding scents.

No wonder dogs were so good at sniffing out prey. Thaddeus could have easily followed the trail of several humans who had come this way and even the faded trail of a few Lycans. But he had no interest in those wolves. The ones he wanted he didn't need to smell, not when he now had a bead on them in his mind.

Closing the lid on the box of ash shut them away but didn't hide their lingering effect. He tossed it in the trunk of his car along with his keys, wallet, and phone. He slammed it and the car door shut then, with a mental flick, engaged the locks.

Time to track down some lost wolves.

Chapter Ten

As if a spectral presence, Marc watched from above, a floating, bodiless entity as a dark-haired man snorted from a box that seemed familiar. *Probably because I saw some vamp dude sweeping Roderick's ashes into it.* With a detached interest, he noted the man's reaction, the way he fell to his knees and struggled to compose himself, as if fighting an inner battle.

Probably allergies given the snort of dust. Or was it something else?

A part of Marc understood he dreamed, yet it didn't detract from the realness of the moment nor the sense of connection he felt toward the vampire who stood and surveyed the area around him, in full control of himself once again and appearing predatory with a glint of red shining in his eyes. The male stripped himself of unneeded items and locked the box in his car before loping off into the woods in search of prey.

Marc's wolf grew agitated.

The hunter is on his way. Evil comes. Danger hunts us. Run. Run now!

Marc bolted upright, breathing hard, his eyes frantically scanning the darkness.

He almost bolted. The instinct to flee on the heels of his strange nightmare was strong. Only the recollection he wasn't alone kept him from engaging in a mad dash into the woods.

Antonia, who'd stopped speaking to him after his announcement of Pack Law, stirred. She whimpered and tossed.

"No," she muttered. "No. He's dead. Evil comes. Must hide. Must run."

Caught in the throes of a nightmare, one too similar to his own he'd wager, he placed a hand on her shoulder and shook her. "Wake up, Toni. It's just a dream."

With a cry, she batted at his hands and scrambled away. Her eyes flashed a feral yellow in the darkness, and her breath emerged in short pants. "Stay away from me," she yelled.

Marc didn't take offense. He would wager she didn't speak to him but the ghost of a dead man returned to haunt them both.

She scrubbed a hand across her face and took a few heaving breaths. "Fuck. What the hell was that?"

"Did you feel it, too?" he whispered. Why the low voice, he couldn't say. He didn't sense an intruder, and yet, he couldn't shake the feeling of menace lurking just out of sight.

"Like something tickled my brain? Yeah. Reminded me of Roderick."

"Only not." Not and yet something about it felt the same. Already he couldn't quite recall it. The ghostly touch on his psyche hadn't lasted long, but that didn't calm the wolf pacing in his head.

Danger. What or where, he couldn't say, but his

gut and his furry side didn't trust the unnatural stillness around them. The forest at night only went silent for one reason alone, and it usually wasn't good.

"I think we need to move," he said, his voice still hushed.

"Not going to hear me argue," she mumbled as she staggered to her feet. Her nude body didn't gleam as brightly as his in the dark. His insanely white complexion just about glowed, making him wish, not for the first time, that he could tan. But then again, how often did he end up naked in the woods at night with the feeling something was watching him from the shadows?

Once was enough.

He didn't like it one bit. Despite her annoyance with him earlier, Antonia followed close behind Marc as he tread carefully in the dark. Their bare feet helped to keep the sound of their passage at a minimum, but they still made too much noise, each crackle of a dry leaf or snap of a twig like a gunshot in the stillness.

Where were the crickets? The usual sounds of the night? Not even a gentle breeze stirred the almost bare branches. It was as if the world held its breath for—

The attack came out of nowhere. One moment, he listened and sniffed, and the next, a shadowy figure launched itself from the branches above him and took him to the ground.

"Fuck!" He cursed aloud, one syllable, which was

all he had the breath for as he scrambled to stay alive.

Teeth gnashed at his face while feral, red eyes pierced him—and shook him to his core.

Oh fuck, it's Roderick. Fear almost froze him, but an instinct for survival, as well as a shriek from Toni, spurred him to fight. He braced his hands against his assailant's shoulders, blocking the blunted chompers from attacking any major veins. However, he couldn't hope to hold the savage monster off for long. As he maneuvered to wedge his knees against the freak's chest, he realized the creature he battled wasn't Roderick. Some sort of vampire, yes, or so he assumed given the eyes, but not the one he feared most. And in a stroke of luck, the rabid bastard wasn't as strong.

With his knees in place, Marc pushed and sent his attacker soaring. It didn't work as well as he would have liked. Instead of the vampire hitting a tree and hurting himself or, even better, impaling him on a jutting limb—which, if this were an action flick, would have totally happened—the fucker twisted in midair and landed on his feet.

The subsequent leer and chuckle, accompanied with the red-eyed stare, was straight out of a B movie, and Marc felt a lot of his initial fear fade. Funny how a man could find courage when least expected. "Really, dude? Could you be any more cliché?" His taunting words bolstered him further. *I can take this prick.*

He heard Toni's gasp, whether at his temerity or

the rushing of the vampire he couldn't have said. But with his new confidence, he met the vampire head-on, grabbing him in a wrestler move, arms locked, feet braced and both of them straining for the upper hand.

He grunted. The creature snarled. Given the stalemate, he wasn't too proud to say, "A little help over here, Toni?"

He couldn't spare a glance her way, not being occupied with the task of staying alive—and in one piece. But it seemed she'd heard his plea because she appeared suddenly behind his foe and brought a rock down hard on its head. It dented the skull, and the vampire's grip loosened.

It didn't stop him.

Marc yelled, "Hit him again."

She would have. Her arm was poised above her head, but the vampire let go of Marc and whirled to grab her. Dammit. *Where is a fucking sword when you need one?*

The vampire ignored Marc to focus his attention on Toni, staring at her with his freaky, red eyes. Her face went slack. Her eyes took on a glazed look. The rock dropped.

Oh shit. Marc used the creature's lack of attention to drop and grab a rock of his own. Maybe if he smashed the skull enough times it would act as a decapitation, the only sure way he knew to kill a vampire and make sure they stayed that way.

Of course, his plan would work only if he managed to hit the fucker. Toni taken care of, in other words, drooling and staring off into space under some kind of mojo spell, the vampire could now devote his entire attention to Marc.

"I don't suppose we could talk."

"I don't talk with household pets," the vampire hissed.

He could have pointed out he just had, but he doubted antagonizing him at this point would really help, not when he could barely breathe as the monster grabbed him by the throat and dangled him off the ground.

How ironic and so like the universe. Give him a few days freedom to regret the things he'd done, give him a chance to redeem himself, then kill him.

At least I tried. Marc just wished he could have done more to help Toni. Poor Toni who was about to end up in the clutches of yet another sadistic bastard.

Not while I'm still alive.

The need to rescue her gave him strength, and he kicked out, trying to break the grasp. His foot connected with a solid thump, but it did nothing to loosen the hold around his neck. His next blow was weaker as the lack of air circulating through his body made his attempts at escape laughable.

Weakness flooded his limbs. Dark spots danced in front of his eyes. A blurring motion made him blink. A sharp *crack* and the hold on him let go. He snapped his eyes open in time to see the ground rushing up to meet his face. Not good.

He opened his mouth to yell and ate dirt. Not

one of his more graceful moments.

And lucky him, one that didn't go unnoticed, according to the mocking comment.

"Don't you wish you'd been born a cat? They, at least, always land on their feet."

Chapter Eleven

The sound of a skirmish wouldn't have usually drawn his attention, not when he hunted other prey. However, Thaddeus noted that at least one of his targets coincided with the noise. He hurried to intercept.

He came across an odd tableaux. To one side stood a lovely Latina, utterly nude, eyes vacant, hair an unbound mess and her easily read mind utterly horrified at having so readily succumbed to a vampire. Across from her, a vampire, a young one by Thaddeus's reckoning, held a wolf by the scruff of his human neck. Feet dangled. Cheeks turned purple. Eyes bulged. The male was in dire need of assistance before he asphyxiated.

Not being the altruistic kind, Thaddeus could have easily grabbed the girl and ignored the others but for a few facts. One, he didn't recognize the vampire. And two, something about the wolf niggled at his mind or, more accurately, niggled the hazy memories he'd acquired from Roderick's ashes.

Bloody hell. He'd have to play the part of rescuer. How annoying—and bad for his reputation if it got out. Thankfully, no one was around to witness.

It took only a quick twist to snap the young vamp's neck. He watched with callous disregard as the corpse fell to the ground but couldn't help a smirk as the naked dog also hit the ground face first, nor could he help his sarcastic remark.

A baleful blue eye in a freckled face turned his way. The dog spat out a mouthful of dirt before replying to his taunt. "Cats scratch."

"So do sexy women," Thaddeus replied, "especially if you make them purr." Speaking of women…He turned on a heel and regarded the lovely Latina as she blinked the effect of the incapacitated vampire away. Her bleary mental state answered one question. Wolves under Roderick's previous influence were now susceptible to enchantment, even from a weak vamp. Not exactly the best of news. It was a good thing he'd arrived when he did to rescue her—and take her as his own.

Intent on examining her, with a lusty interest he'd not experienced in a while, Thaddeus missed spotting the fist that connected with his jaw. It didn't hurt, but the force behind it sent him staggering, and irritated him.

"Leave her alone," growled the redhead, who Thaddeus now regretted saving. How dare the canine interfere in his business!

Turning to direct the full impact of his stare on the presumptuous mutt, he met the rage-filled glare with his red-tinged one. "Behave, dog, before I have you neutered. What I do with this female is of no concern to you."

"I will not fucking behave. She's been through enough without another one of you bloodsuckers picking up where Roderick left off."

"She won't come to any harm with me. On the contrary, I intend to bring her much pleasure." Bathe her, perfume her, and splay her on a bed of fine silk for feasting. Hunger of two kinds stirred within him. Thaddeus couldn't wait to exit this filthy forest with his treasure and escape the fast approaching dawn.

"I'll kill you first," threatened the wolf, fists clenched at his side, his body poised for a fight.

Thaddeus resisted the urge to roll his eyes. It was undignified at his age. "You are trying my patience. Don't make me spell you. Just keep your mouth shut and you'll come to no harm. I have no quarrel with you. I seek only to corral those Roderick has touched."

"We have no interest in being corralled. We're not bloody cattle."

Ah, so the pup was one of Roderick's minions. Odd how he didn't feel him like he felt the girl. "You might not be on the menu for dinner, but you are annoying. Don't say I didn't warn you. I think it's time someone muzzled you." *Hold your tongue.* Thaddeus held the red-haired wolf's stare and imbued his order with power. He pushed his will at the dog. The dog didn't shut his mouth. Didn't obey. Hell, he didn't even blink.

"Muzzle me? I'd like to see you try."

Thaddeus frowned. Why didn't it work? He tried again. "I said to shut your annoying mouth." Again, he threw his power of persuasion at the wolf. Threw it and got nowhere. Damned wolf. Apparently this wolf hadn't fallen under Roderick's influence like the girl, which meant he had no use for him. He'd have to get rid of him the hard way, but it seemed a shame to kill him for acting chivalrous. *Perhaps I'll just take the girl and leave. I can move faster than him.*

But of course, the girl couldn't just let him sling her over a shoulder without making a fuss.

"Put me down," she shrieked, pounding at his back.

"Put her down," the mutt said, also hitting him.

Thaddeus got annoyed. "Enough!" he yelled. His voice boomed and echoed, the strength in that one word command almost visible.

To his shock it had an effect. The female stopped her fighting and even the wolf halted his fist mid-strike, his jaw open wide in disbelief. It lasted only a moment, but apparently the fact he could do it meant something.

The redhead backed up and whispered, "How did you do that?"

"It's called speech. You know, words that convey meaning."

The dog shook his head. "Not that. The alpha command. The way you just spoke right now. It's a wolf thing, but you're not a wolf. The only other people I ever saw do that was my old pack leader and Roderick."

Of course. Roderick. Yet another Lycan advantage. The danger posed by those ashes grew by leaps and bounds. Questions mounted. Just what else were Lycans capable of? What other surprises might be in store? Thaddeus didn't know, but he needed answers. Lucky for him, he had two possible sources in front of him.

Given he needed them alive, and they wouldn't cooperate, he'd have to—ugh—negotiate. "If I promise to leave the girl alone, will you come with me and answer some questions?"

"As if your promise means anything."

"Are you calling my word into doubt?" How astonishing. The wolf already knew him so well, and on such a short acquaintance.

"I've dealt with a vampire before. I know you're lying, sadistic bastards."

Finally, an intelligent mutt. "Some. Not all. And believe it or not, I am in these woods to make sure the rotten ones don't become the majority. But much as it galls me to admit, I need help and information. From you." He couldn't help his distaste.

"What if I don't want to help?"

"Are all your kind so bloody annoying? I'm trying to prevent a mass extinction of your kind, and yet you Lycans keep insisting on being stubborn as mules. I tire of this. If you don't want to help me, I'll find another. So make up your mind. Are you coming with me or not? Because if not, then I'll just take the girl and go. The sun is coming, and much like you and your fair skin, its rays are not my friend."

The red-haired wolf snorted. "I hardly call a

sunburn on my lily-white skin the same, seeing as how you turn into campfire dust. But I guess I don't have many options. You promise not to hurt us?" Blue eyes met his with serious intent.

Thaddeus replied in kind, "I won't hurt you." Seduce the girl, and possibly kill the redhead once he didn't need him? Yes, but he'd make it quick and painless. So not entirely a lie.

The mutt nodded, despite the female's gasped, "Marc, no. Don't believe him."

"Hush, woman." It only took a quick glance her way to quiet her. At least his power worked on her. He turned back to the male. "Glad we're agreed. I'll carry the woman, but I need you to do me a favor. Bring the body of our dead friend there, would you? His injury is only temporary, and while I doubt he'll recover before sunrise, we wouldn't want to accidentally turn some cuddly forest creatures into blood-sucking freaks."

"You're kidding, right?" the Marc fellow asked.

"Of course." Thaddeus smiled wide, too wide, and watched the other man swallow hard before leaning to pick up the body. As for the woman, she might not have the power to speak aloud, but Thaddeus had access to her mind, which muttered, "Men."

Ah, a female with spirit. This hunt just got more and more interesting.

Chapter Twelve

Despite Toni's feelings on the matter, Marc chose to trust the domineering vampire. Personally, Toni would have liked to kick him in the shin just to see him dance around looking like an idiot. Or, at the very least, slap the condescending smirk off his face, a good-looking face that went well with his obviously fit body. Things she really shouldn't have noticed but couldn't seem to ignore, especially once the vampire swept her into his arms.

Carried like a princess, his command to stay quiet held, and with nothing better to do, she couldn't help but reflect on the next fucked-up episode of her life.

Am I delirious?

Perhaps she'd not really escaped her cell at all. Maybe she languished in a coma-like state, experiencing realistic illusions as her body waited for death to claim her. What else but a dream could explain the craziness that kept multiplying? As if events until that point weren't nuts enough, now she could add attacked by a vampire who, in turn, was killed by another, who then proceeded to carry her out of the woods at a breakneck speed.

And what if she didn't imagine it? What if this was all real? *Hello, straitjacket and padded cell.*

Because her new supernatural life wasn't the

most messed-up part of it all. Nope, the part that totally made her believe she'd gone around the bend was the fact that she couldn't help but find the bloodsucking, violent asshat carrying her attractive.

Who thought about licking a strange guy's neck when he was practically kidnapping her? She did, apparently, and licking wasn't all she wanted to do. The *other* in her head kept putting images of her biting the tempting column.

Bite? She, who hated hickeys and who couldn't fathom leaving scratches on anyone's back, bite someone?

I think my experiences have left me completely unbalanced. How else to explain the wild fantasies she couldn't seem to halt? How else to explain how her heart raced as he carried her and her body flushed with heat?

Great. Just great. First she'd found herself eying her werewolf savior and fighting an urge to nibble at his skin. Now, she wanted to seduce a vampire. She truly had turned into a slutty Bella.

Thankfully, no one noticed her inappropriate attraction. She hoped. With her new heightened senses, she could smell her arousal. Did that mean Marc with his wolfy sense of smell could too?

Better not to dwell on it or her mortification level would probably cause her to self-combust. Instead, she'd think about where they were going and why. The vampire seemed to want them for something, something that concerned Roderick. Perhaps he had questions about what Roderick had been up to in his final days. Or was he looking to tie up loose ends? His words in regards to her implied seduction, but she didn't put much credence in them. What man, even a vampire, in his right mind would lust after an unwashed, wild-haired, howling-at-the-moon gal?

Marc wanted her. Despite his many attempts, he'd not managed to hide the evidence of his attraction, but being a gentleman, he didn't act on it. Somehow she doubted the vampire would show the same restraint. She shivered, but she couldn't have said whether it was in trepidation he would or anticipation.

I need to think about something else. Such as his promise that he wouldn't hurt them. Did he mean it?

So far he'd not physically harmed her, but on the other hand, he'd compelled her to stay quiet. Was this what she had to look forward to? One look in his eyes and she turned into a mindless slave, her body ready and willing to do his bidding? *Hell, if he wants my body, he could just ask or touch. I seem more than willing to turn to putty in his hands.*

It took far less time for them to exit the woods than she would have thought. She'd imagined herself days from civilization, but given the distance she and Marc traveled before settling down for the night and the vampire's breakneck speed, which Marc, with his heavy burden had a hard time following, they emerged in a parking lot before the dawn started to tinge the sky.

Marc dumped the body on the asphalt as the

vampire set her on her feet. She wobbled at the sudden change, and two sets of male hands grabbed and steadied her. She sucked in a breath as calloused fingers on her waist and smooth ones at the small of her back contrasted on her bare skin. She really needed to better control her hypersensitivity to these guys. A result of her new wolf side or her hormones acting up? Either way, something was saying "Hey, isn't it time you indulged in a little something-something?"

Down, girl. She used the jest in her mind, aimed at herself, but was surprised to sense the *other* grumble in discontent and even more disconcerted at the faint male laughter she thought she could hear.

"This is my car," the vamp announced. Without the use of a key, not one she saw at any rate, the trunk to the dark sedan they stood beside popped open. Her abductor leaned in and pulled out some items; keys, wallet, phone. He also retrieved a coat from under an ornate box and tossed it at her.

Grateful for the warmth and cover, she quickly slipped it on, and the spicy scent of cologne and man, plus something a little darker, enveloped her.

"Got anything for me?" Marc asked, legs akimbo and still unabashedly nude.

"I will at the hotel. I did not realize I would require attire, or I would have come better prepared."

"Hotel?" Marc arched a brow. "And how do you figure on sneaking me in? I'm pretty sure they won't let a six-foot naked guy waltz through their front doors."

"I'm sure we will figure something out." Somehow the vampire's reassuring smile did the opposite.

Antonia shivered. If ever a man looked dangerous, he did.

"Get in the car. We need to make it to my quarters before the sun rises."

"Not fond of barbecue?" Once again, Marc baited him.

"About as much as you'd be fond of a silver bullet."

Antonia stored that interesting tidbit. So part of the legends were true. Silver and werewolves didn't mix.

The passenger door opened, aided by the same ghostly hands that popped the trunk. Did the vampire possess magic? Antonia wasn't quite brave enough to ask, but she did slide into the vehicle without hesitation. She wasn't stupid. Given her current situation, she knew better than to try and run. Besides, where would she run to?

It didn't take a genius to assess the situation. It could be summed up in one word: dire. Wearing a coat, with nothing underneath, no ID, no money, and no access to a phone, she was in a tough spot. Asking anyone for help would mean making herself vulnerable.

Vampires and werewolves weren't the only ones to fear. Women could never take too many precautions, not with the many predators humanity boasted.

Beside, some of the things Marc had said during their trek had time to ferment. Or at least raised questions. What did she really know about her new Lycan heritage? What would it mean to her, and what about her family? What could she tell them? How would she cope? She needed to know more before making any decisions about her future. Although his assertion she'd be subject to Pack rules, including the one about her taking on more than one guy? Yeah, so not happening. Her mother would disown her for sure if she did.

Not to mention, it just wasn't done. *I mean, really. One guy is tough enough to keep satisfied, how the hell would I manage two?*

For some reason the sudden vivid image of her caught between two male bodies, their naked skin rubbing against hers, their hands roaming, their lips kissing, their…

She pinched herself and put a halt to the taboo thoughts, ideas she was sure the wolf in her head planted because she would never indulge in that kind of decadence. Ever. Even if it seemed fun.

The rear end of the car dipped as they heaved the dead body into it and then slammed the trunk shut. Marc slid into the seat beside her while the vampire took the driver's spot, the box she'd spotted in the trunk placed on the passenger seat, something about it drawing her eye.

What's in it?

She didn't ask, but she did pray she'd survive the

trip as the car sped off with a squeal of tires.

The vampire drove with reckless abandon, taking corners sharply and at high speeds. The slippery leather seats in the back made keeping her balance hard, especially since she'd neglected to buckle herself in. A bad habit she really should rectify if she was going to get in cars driven by someone with aspirations of NASCAR racing.

After the second time she slammed into Marc, he solved the problem by putting his arm around her and hugging her to his body. She should have protested, or moved away, but the warmth of his presence soothed her. It gave her the false impression of protection. She also liked the way his bare thigh rubbed along hers.

"How are you doing?" he asked in a low voice.

She hesitated to speak, wondering if the vampire still had her muted by his command, but it seemed he'd either removed the compulsion or it had worn off. "Good, I guess. Not great, but better than I was a few days ago. Could be worse. At least we didn't end up dinner for that other guy."

He chuckled wryly. "I guess that's one way of looking at it. But still, I'm sorry we got caught again. This wasn't part of my plan."

"I don't think anything that's happened to us recently was. I suppose I'm going to have to get used to having vampires and werewolves popping into my life on a regular basis now. Maybe I should also prepare for a few zombies and demons."

She'd thought their vampire driver ignored them,

but he interjected at this point. "Zombies are rare and require great power to summon. Demons are banned from this plane."

"Well, that's good to know. Any other mythical creatures I should watch out for?" She peered into the rearview mirror and caught his gaze, as well as the tilt of his lips. Warmth curled low in her belly. *Figures the devil would be much too handsome.*

"A few, but most shy away from contact outside their race."

"How is it no one suspects you and the wolves and all these other creatures really do exist?" Sure, the rag magazines screamed it, but no one paid attention to those.

"Oh, people suspect. They just can't seem to find proof. We are very good at hiding our traces."

"The Pack Laws are very strict on breaches," Marc added.

"Strict how?" she asked.

The vampire laughed. "Go on, tell her, dog. There's only one sure way to keep a secret."

The implication didn't escape her. Disturbed, and now worried, she diverted her attention by asking a question. "So I have to ask, that is if me talking won't get us slammed into a telephone pole, what do you want with us?"

Again, husky laughter bathed her in a rich vibration that she felt from her toes up. "I assure you my reflexes are more than adequate for this vehicle. And as to your query, I need you for numerous reasons. The foremost being to keep you from the clutches of other vampires who would use you to further their own agenda."

"Like we're not pawns in yours?" Marc replied sarcastically.

"I never said you weren't. Right now, any wolf touched by Roderick is vulnerable. Their minds, having been overtaken once, are extremely susceptible now to all of my kind."

"I wasn't," Marc boasted.

"Only Roderick's minions will have this issue; other wolves won't. We believe it was the fact Roderick began as a Lycan and a strong alpha that allowed him to mesmerize so many. Usually your kind is impervious to our mental touch."

"So you mean I can be any vampire's toy?" Antonia didn't like this at all. She shivered, and Marc hugged her tighter.

"Only if you are unclaimed."

"What does unclaimed mean?"

"If another vampire chooses to make you his or her thrall, then you will be safe from others."

"But still a slave to a vampire. Isn't there a way to skip that part?" She couldn't help the lower lip jutting with her question. Dammit. It seemed so unfair.

"Not all vampires are sadistic like Roderick. Many are good and fair masters who treat their thralls well. Very well actually. It is much easier to survive when surrounded by people with a vested interest in keeping you alive than by those who'd prefer to see you dead."

"Speaking of dead, who was that vampire in the woods, the one we've got stuffed in the trunk?" Marc adeptly changed the subject.

"I don't know, which is troublesome."

"Why? I mean it's not as if you'd know all the vampires in the world. Or do you?"

"No, I do not. I probably shouldn't relay this, however, our numbers are not as many as you'd think. The creation of vampires is not an easy process, even with humans. It's almost impossible with Lycans. So if I were to return to your initial question, yes, in a sense, we are very much aware of each other. And when it comes to this territory, I should know all who trespass. Those visiting are supposed to declare themselves before the council for the region."

"And I take it this vamp didn't?"

"No. I also don't know why he was in those woods and why he was hunting you, although I do have my suspicions. I'm just surprised Morpheus would be so clumsy in his choice of hunters."

"Who's Morpheus?" she asked.

"An enemy of mine, and yours."

"Says you." Marc's fingers danced along the back of her neck, tickling her as he baited the vampire into telling them more. "How do we know you're not the bad guy? I mean you snapped that other guy's neck without even thinking twice."

The car slammed to a halt, jolting them and rattling her teeth, but her sudden spurt of fear had little to do with their arrival and more with what their vampire said next. "Morpheus would make the world into his hunting and feeding ground. You would do well to fear, as he plans to eradicate your pack. And he plans to do so using you and your lady friend as cannon fodder."

Chapter Thirteen

Arriving at the hotel didn't bring him any relief. Something bothered Thaddeus, and it wasn't the comatose vampire in his trunk or the naked werewolf in his backseat or even the impending sunrise. It centered around the conversation he'd had with his passengers and their allusion they were both thralls to Roderick.

And yet only the girl succumbed to my persuasion. Why?

The male, Marc, was a beta. No doubt about it. Yes, he did bear some strength of spirit and mind, especially when it came to the girl, but when it all boiled down, he wasn't the commanding type. So, if he'd been one of Roderick's minions, how did he manage to fight Thaddeus's compulsion? What made him special? And could Thaddeus use it to foil Morpheus's plot to use the wolves to start a war?

I must find out how Marc has protected his mind from compulsion. But first, he needed to get them behind closed doors and thick drapes before the sun's irritatingly bright rays made their appearance over the horizon.

Getting Marc into the hotel, clothed, proved easy. Thaddeus simply convinced a traveler about to leave the hotel to catch a flight to open his luggage and hand over some of his clothes. At this time of day, or night, the staff were few, and using his keycard at the more discreet parking lot entrance and the stairs, they managed to evade notice as they made their way to the penthouse level.

In hiding or not, only the best would do, under an assumed name, of course, and via the liberal application of bribery and mesmerizing. *Just because I'm hunted doesn't mean I can't still enjoy comfort.*

The first thing Thaddeus did upon entering the suite was to scout his temporary domain, searching for signs of an intruder. With his new olfactory senses, it proved easy. No vampires other than him had crossed the threshold. Good.

As per his instructions, the hotel staff had drawn the drapes tight in the main room, their blackout lining blocking the impending morning sun. He wouldn't turn to ash this day.

Now on to a more pressing matter, securing his guests so he could safely slumber and recoup some strength while the sun cast its evil glare upon the earth. How he wished at times he'd never left the marshy Highlands with its misty grey days. Perhaps once he'd foiled Morpheus's plot he'd return. He still held rights to a castle overseas. *I wonder what the girl will think of the moors?*

Which brought him back around to thoughts of *her*. The she-wolf intrigued him, and yet he couldn't pinpoint why. The outer packaging was attractive, but definitely not model beautiful. Even though she'd obviously lost some weight during her incarceration, she'd quickly put it back on with a few good meals he'd wager. Her hips were the type usually well padded, her buttocks plentiful, her skin tanned and clear, her lips lush and full, her eyes both vulnerable and feisty. A true Latina type.

His usual preference when it came to bedsport was petite, blonde, and preferably AB Rh negative, the rarest of bloods and thus considered a delicacy among his kind. Knowing his predilection, why this sudden urge for something a little more voluptuous and exotic? He barely knew the chit, yet already he mentally planned to take her abroad? Perhaps Roderick's ashes had done more to him than increase his power base.

He'd have to worry about it later. The sun hovered on the horizon, and he needed to attend to his dilemma of how to contain his guests. He could persuade the girl, but how to ensure the male didn't flee, dragging her along with him?

"Nice place." Marc paced the outer edges of the room, alert and marking out the confines of his temporary territory. At least he didn't cock a leg and pee.

"It's adequate for the moment." More of a four star rather than his usual luxurious five but convenient to his purpose. "I will take the master bedroom for myself. You and the girl may share the other."

Despite having already drawn the drapes, Thaddeus still felt the rising of the sun. But even knowing those disgusting cheerful rays bathed the window, he didn't flinch as the wolf paused his pacing to stand in front of curtains.

"So what now?"

"Now, I rest. You should too. When I rise, we shall speak more of Roderick and the wolves under his dominion, as well as plan a strategy for finding the others."

"You're going to bed?" Incredulity marked the male's tone. "Like fuck. No way you're going to trust us to not stake you in your sleep."

Thaddeus gave him a tired smile. "Go ahead. You wouldn't be the first to try and die. But keep in mind, if you fail, that leaves the girl alone. Vulnerable. To me. Others. Do you really want that?"

"What makes you think we won't just disappear then? Hide where you can't find us."

Thaddeus couldn't help his laughter. "Hide? Wolf, there is nowhere you could hide that I wouldn't find. I was born to hunt. To kill. And kill you I shall if you waste my time with petty games. But, again, feel free to choose your own path. If you'd prefer to choose the harder path, then by all means do so. Just keep in mind you could do worse than be my guests."

"And how do we know you're the lesser of the evils?" Antonia asked, looking utterly scrumptious in his coat, her bare legs peeking from the hem, her bountiful breasts creating a delectable shadowy hollow in the vee above the button at the waist.

He'd explore that temptation later, once he'd rested and gotten some answers—as well as a better handle on his rioting emotions and urges. He needed time to assimilate Roderick's powers. "Such distrustful souls. Let me ask, have I done anything to harm you? On the contrary, I saved you from sure death or torture. I haven't fed on you, even though I'm craving a bite. And yet you still want to aggravate the only person protecting you right now. Are you both that stupid? Then I dare you. Go ahead. But keep in mind that in doing so you doom many to death and horror."

"You keep referring to some dire event but have yet to explain it."

"And I'm not going to start now. If you want details, you'll have to wait until sundown. Until then, my suspicious companions, *bonum nocte*." With a bow and a mocking smile, Thaddeus took himself to his bedroom, closed the door and locked it.

He stripped and slipped into bed, keeping on a pair of briefs. It had taken only one fight in the buff to realize that dangling parts were distracting in a fight, and undignified. As he pillowed an arm under his head, he wondered if he should have ordered the girl to join him.

Toni. Her name is Toni. He'd picked that much up during the light forays he'd made into her thoughts. He knew she resented the intrusion, but he couldn't help but peek, especially once he scented her arousal. The musky scent, so sweet, so tempting, had him needing to know whom she craved. To his irritation, while he occupied a large portion of her thoughts, he shared them with the mangy mutt.

A mutt who was currently making a move on *his*

woman. Thaddeus didn't stop to examine his actions. He sprang from bed, determined to put a stop it.

Chapter Fourteen

From naked in the woods to partially clothed in luxury. Once again, her fucked-up life had taken another twist.

How much more could she take?

Antonia stood in her borrowed coat amidst the lavish decor and felt the energy ebb from her. Her limbs trembled. Her lip quivered. She blinked back tears.

Marc noticed her slow-motion breakdown and moved quickly to grasp her hands, attempting to reassure her. "Hey now. What's this? No crying. Not now. You're safe."

"Or not. You heard the vampire. More shit is about to rain down on us because of our association with Roderick. Will I never be free? Am I forever damned to get passed from one vampire to the next?" *Although at least this one I can stomach. For now. How attractive will he seem if he starts to abuse me?*

"You don't have to stay here if you don't feel safe. We can leave."

"And go where?" was her almost hysterical reply. "Should I go back home and possibly put my family in jeopardy if these vampires decide to follow? Should I join your so-called Pack where they'll let some strangers *claim me*—she made finger quotes—because of their archaic laws? Yeah, I want to live somewhere where overbearing men will tell me what I can or can't do and where my only worth is in popping out babies. Or do I stay here and hope this vampire, who never even gave us his fucking name, won't decide to turn me into his next toy? If you ask me, I don't have much of a choice."

"At least if I took you to the nearest pack, you wouldn't have to deal with vampires."

A brittle laugh escaped her. "Says you. You saw how easily he compelled me. How can your Pack protect me from that, short of locking me up for my own good?"

"I don't know, but they'd try."

"And let's say they succeed and the vampires go away. What then? Will they let me leave if I'm not happy? Can you promise they won't force me to mate because of their stupid laws?" She searched his face for reassurance and found none.

He clamped his lips and didn't reply.

She pulled away from him and gestured wildly. "See what I mean? I'm fucked. And not in a good way." A grimace crossed her features.

"Is your only problem with joining a Pack the whole mating thing?"

"Only? Only!" Her voice rose to a shrill shriek. She couldn't help it. His nonchalance bothered her. "Isn't that enough? How would you like it if someone told you that you'd have to marry a bloody stranger? Make that two or more?"

"What if I had a solution?"

"What kind of solution? Got a silver bullet

handy?" She knew she didn't mean it as soon as the words left her lips, but he didn't. The shock on his face was genuine.

"Suicide isn't the answer. And I can't believe you'd even think of it. You're too strong for that. You can't give up now after all you've been through."

A sigh made her shoulders sag in defeat. "I didn't mean it. And you're right. I'm not ready to stop fighting yet, but I wish I didn't have to fight. I'd like go to sleep and pretend none of this happened, that I'll wake up in my own bed, a normal girl, rushing to get to work and grumbling to my coworkers about the weather and our lousy pay."

"And you can have that again." He seemed so earnest, so convinced. If only she could believe it, but somewhere along the way, she'd lost hope. It was easier to imagine the worst. Then, no matter what, nothing seemed as bad.

"I'll never have my old life again. You told me so yourself. I'm part wolf now. It changes everything."

"It does, and it doesn't. Just because you now have a wolf side to deal with doesn't mean you can't lead a normal life, or as normal as you can expect considering you'll need to let your other half run free a time or two a month to stay sane."

"But only if I join a Pack and follow your stupid laws." In the end, it all circled back to the same problem.

"Our laws are pretty simple. Mostly they involve don't tell anyone about us and marry a wolf."

"Or two. Or more. Kind of makes me wonder if I wouldn't be better off with the vampire. I get the impression he probably has a harem of women." The wolf in her head growled. "I'd probably only have to deal with him a few times a week, if that."

His eyes widened. "You can't be serious. You'd choose a bloodsucker over your own kind?"

"Your own kind helped Roderick keep me captive, or have you forgotten?" she snapped. Dirty bastards, all of them, leering, touching, pinching, taunting. In some respects, they made her imprisonment worse than the monster himself.

"I can't excuse what they did. Or what I did." His head swung down, and he spoke in a low, regretful voice. "All I can do is atone, starting with you. Let me help you with the Pack."

"How?" He obviously didn't have the power to bend the laws for her, or he would have already offered.

"I'll be your mate."

It took her a moment to grasp his words. She eyed him up and down in his ill-fitting, borrowed clothes. Sure, he was handsome in a rugged, boy-next-door kind of way. Sure, she'd had some dirty thoughts since she met him… Was it only twenty-four hours or so ago? God, it seemed like an eternity given all that'd happened. Still, though, she wasn't a one-night-stand whore. "You know, I took you for a good guy, but I guess you're like all the rest, wanting to use me."

His brow creased. "What? No, you

misunderstand."

"You just said you wanted to claim me, as your mate, which, if I remember my paranormal lore right, means marriage, which means sex. I barely know you. Why the hell would I agree to something like that?" She planted her hands on her hips and shot him a challenging stare.

Embarrassment on a redhead led to ruddy cheeks, and while the color wasn't attractive, the fact that he could blush and duck his head and stare at his restless feet was. "I wasn't suggesting—That is—" He let out a heavy sigh. "Listen, I wasn't offering so I could get in your pants."

"I'm not wearing pants."

Wow, amazing how his pale skin could turn a brighter hue than his hair. He cleared his throat. "I, um, that is, I wasn't offering as a way of getting sex. What I'm suggesting was a bite exchange."

"What would that do?"

"In our world, it's seen as a mating mark. The exchange of blood and saliva between two Lycans of the opposite sex creates a type of bond, a mating bond. It's how women used to get trapped in claimings. You don't have to have sex to do it, although I hear it makes it more pleasant. Just a bite between us will do the trick."

"You really don't paint a pleasant picture of pack life if women can be forced like that."

"That doesn't really happen anymore. Especially not in the well-run packs."

"But it could."

He nodded. Brownie points for him. He didn't lie to placate her.

"So, what you're saying is you want to bite me. And have me bite you. This helps how? I thought you said the law was two or more."

"It is, but, with at least one, there might be less pressure on you to jump right into a second, especially given how new you are to the whole Lycan deal."

"And what do you get out of it?"

"What do you mean?"

"You're in effect marrying a woman who won't have sex with you." At least not quite yet. She'd perhaps insist on a few dates and dinner first. Or at the very least a shower.

He shrugged. "I won't lie and say I wouldn't like to be your lover. I'm extremely attracted to you. I would hope in time that, perhaps, we could become something more. But if we don't, then that's your choice. Twenty-four hours ago, I was just about ready to give up living. Then I met you. Now, I'm not so keen on throwing in the towel. I'm beginning to wonder if perhaps there's a way I can make amends for what I've done and start over. Maybe hope for a future."

"A future with me? The girl who's done nothing but hassle you since we met. You do remember I kicked you in the balls when you told me about the whole ménage thing, right?"

His lips curved into a smile, and his eyes twinkled in a way she'd come to enjoy since meeting him. "Would you believe the fact you've still got the spunk to fight back after what you've been through is what I find most appealing?"

"Yeah, because it wasn't my naked boobs or fat bottom keeping your attention." As soon as she said it, she realized how it sounded. *What is wrong with me? Am I now fishing for compliments?* Appalled, she stared at her dirty, bare toes.

"The packaging is nice. Very nice." He tilted her chin, forcing her to meet his gaze. "But I'm thinking it's what's inside the package that's gorgeous. And the more I see, the more that belief is reinforced."

"Says a man who's not really seen me lose my temper."

"But has seen you come out of an awful situation with spirit and courage."

"Who smells like a gym sock left in a bag too long."

"Like I said, it's not just the outside I see. I. See. You." He angled his head, and his lips brushed hers. A light, fleeting kiss. One that ignited something in her.

Given all that had happened and still remained unclear, she should have pushed him away, slapped him or kneed him again in the groin. But there was something about the contact, something about the spark it lit, a sense of rightness, a flare of passion, and a need to feel…alive.

I survived. Maybe, despite everything, it's time I celebrated that fact.

Before she could change her mind, she flung her

arms around his neck. Her mouth opened, and she took what he seemed so hesitant to give. She embraced him with the fervor of a woman who didn't know what tomorrow might bring and wanted to take all the pleasure she could find now.

His hesitant kiss evolved. His hands caressed the length of her back. His tongue stroked hers. His heart raced in time to hers, the evidence of his arousal pressed against her, and her sex replied in kind with a low pulse and increasing heat.

I'm alive. And feeling pretty damned good. Even better if—

How far things might have progressed she'd never find out because it took only the mockingly said, "Really, couldn't you have at least showered first before deciding to christen the living room?" to split Toni and Marc apart.

Her heart raced, her cheeks flushed, and her lips tingled, as a part of her yearned to continue the embrace—excited by the prospect of a spectator—while another part felt as if she'd gotten caught cheating. Cheating on the vampire?

She owed him nothing. There was nothing for her to feel guilty about. She tossed her hair back and prepared to give him a tongue lashing—verbal, not physical. Eyeing her dark abductor, leaning against the frame of his bedroom door, clad in tight black briefs and nothing else, his smooth, pale skin showing off a lean musculature, she couldn't help the pulse of excitement between her legs. Her words of chastisement fled her lips. Words of invitation hovered. Shock kept them from being vocalized.

Solid and earthy Marc scowled at the cool and lean vampire. While they engaged in a staring match—which might possibly involve dicks whipping out for measurement of who was the bigger man—she left to find a shower…and her mind.

Chapter Fifteen

If ever Marc wanted to kill somebody, now was the time. Getting interrupted while embracing the most intriguing and beautiful woman he'd ever met, a woman who gave him hope for a future, brought out the savage in him and the jealous beast, especially when he noted Toni's interest in the vampire, an interest he wanted all for his own.

As if sensing the male testosterone levels rising, Toni fled the scene, leaving behind a sexually frustrated wolf.

"I thought you were going to sleep," Marc snarled.

"It occurred to me that I didn't warn you not to let anyone into the room. Visitors should be treated as possible enemies."

"Bullshit. You didn't come out to tell me that. You wanted to interrupt my kiss with Toni."

Dark eyes met his. "And if I did? The woman is vulnerable. You were taking advantage of it. Cajoling her into accepting you as a mate to protect her from your outdated Pack laws? Really?" The vamp shook his head as he tsked. "How rakish of you."

"My intentions are honorable."

"And yet, despite offering her a sexless mating, you kissed her." The vampire arched a brow. "Is it me, or doesn't that fly in the face of your assertion?"

"I did it to make her feel better."

The vamp snorted. "Of course you did."

"Listen, bloodsucker—"

"My name is Thaddeus."

"Well, excuse me, *Thad*. Toni's been through a lot. Add to that she's now a Lycan, and she needs friends right now. Wolf friends, not some dude who messes with her mind."

"Is that what bothers you? That I can compel her?"

"It's not right. Especially if you use it to get her to hop into bed with you." The wolf within him growled, the idea of sharing Toni not sitting well at all. *But is it just because Thad is a vampire? Pack law says I have to share her.*

For the first time since telling her about it, he managed to see it from her point of view. Fuck the whole sharing-was-caring thing. With his two best friends already mated, Marc didn't know of anyone else he'd want to share that kind of lifetime commitment with. Correction, he didn't want to share Toni.

"What if I gave my word not to use my mind tricks to seduce her? What if she came to me willingly?"

"It will never happen." Marc stated it with more confidence than he felt. He wasn't an idiot. Beside the suave vampire, he looked like the ugly duckling or, in this case, wolfling. He couldn't win in a war of looks or charm. *But I am the nicer guy. More human guy. Maybe that will count for something.*

"Is that a challenge?"

"It's a fact." Marc didn't look away even though the vampire did his best to unnerve him with his dark-eyed stare.

"We'll see." With that enigmatic statement, the vampire turned on his heel and returned to his chamber, this time leaving his door unlocked.

Tempting Marc to do something stupid? Or dismissing him as a threat?

Either way, he didn't care. The fatigue of the past few days crashed down on him. While the lure of a shower made him hesitate, he didn't think he could wait while Toni finished luxuriating in hers. Shedding the uncomfortable garments, he stretched out on the couch, the room warm enough, the cushions soft enough, to drag him down into slumber.

And more prophetic dreams.

Chapter Sixteen

The stone block walls of the cell taunted her.

No. How did I get back here? I escaped.

Or had she? Had her meeting with Marc and the vampire only been a dream?

Dammit. No. It couldn't be. She remembered things too clearly. Even she didn't have the imagination to conjure them up in such vivid dreaming color. Not to mention, she refused to lose hope, a hope that blossomed, especially after Marc's kiss. A real kiss or a mirage? How could she tell?

The last thing she remembered was showering, the scalding-hot water sluicing the filth of her ordeal from her skin. The hotel soap, and its fresh scent, cleansed her, leaving her lightly perfumed. With a towel wrapped around her hair and another around her body, she recalled peeking into the living room. Marc snored lightly on the couch, his splayed, nude body a temptation she almost gave in to. She wouldn't have minded someone to hold her as she slept, to whisper everything would be all right.

But she didn't give in to the weakness. She was safe for the moment, if by safe she didn't dwell on the fact a vampire slept in one room and a werewolf in the other. The new normal for her life. One she'd have to get used to.

No use in dwelling on it. A fluffy bed with clean

sheets called her.

Last thing she recalled her head hit the pillow and she'd closed her eyes and…dreamed she was back in her cell.

This must be a nightmare. Had to be. And if this was a product of her mind, then that meant she controlled it. With that belief firmly entrenched, she strode to the door and yanked. The heavy portal didn't budge.

She pulled again, belief turning to panic. *Nooooo!*

Pounding on the door, she yelled, "Let me out! Goddamn you, I won't be a prisoner again."

Unlike the last time she cried for help, someone answered her call. She managed to stumble in retreat only moments before the door swung open. A tall dark figure bathed in shadows filled the doorway.

Who stood there?

The first thing she noticed was the red eyes. Glowing eyes. She moaned a fearful, "Roderick."

The menacing shape took a step into the cell, and terror melted as she beheld the vampire's face. Not Roderick, and yet, something about him, something about his presence, his aura, was darkly familiar. The chiseled features of her abductor were anything but evil, though, and she couldn't help a spurt of happiness he'd answered her call. Her vampire savior back again to the rescue or her new jailor?

"Don't fear. It's me, Thaddeus."

An interesting name, old-fashioned and yet it suited him. "Why am I here? Why have you brought me back? Marc said he burned this place down. How is this possible?"

He arched a brow. "Me? I did nothing. I've never visited this dismal location before. I'm afraid this setting is of your doing. You drew me into your dream."

"So this isn't real?" He inclined his head, and she heaved a sigh of relief. "Thank God. Once I escaped, I prayed I'd never have to go back."

"Neither prayer nor God has anything to do with it. My understanding is your will kept you alive until the wolf released you."

"But who led him to me in the first place?" she sassed back. Look at her, arguing theology with a vampire.

Thaddeus laughed. "A question scholars could debate for centuries and never come to an agreement."

"Whatever the reason, I'm glad I escaped."

"As am I."

"I find that hard to believe. Why would you care?"

Thaddeus stepped farther into the cell, a frown knitting his brow as he glanced around the miserable room. "What Roderick did to you was vile, even by vampire standards."

"How would you know? I haven't told you anything." And didn't plan to. That part of her life was best left in the past, locked away and forgotten.

"You might not have said anything, but I've seen glimpses of it in your mind and from the memories

I've ingested."

"Double whoa. What do you mean by seen it and ingested?"

He turned his attention from the cold stone blocks and focused his gaze on her. "Because you were once in thrall to Roderick, your mind is similar to an open book, easy to read for those of us with the power to do so."

She grimaced. "Great. Nothing like having your worst moments on display."

"Your secrets are safe with me."

"I'd prefer you not have them at all. Isn't there a way of closing the journal of my life?" Before Thaddeus got to the part where she found him attractive. *Don't think of it. Quick, hide that thought.* She shoved it behind a door in her mind and locked it. "Isn't there a mind trick I can learn to prevent you from reading it?"

"I'm afraid the only way you could close yourself off, at least to others, would be to become a thrall once again."

Not the answer she'd hoped for. Her lips twisted into a moue of displeasure. "You mean become a slave to a vampire."

"Not all of us treat humans with disdain. Some are cherished companions. Friends. Even lovers." He flashed a seductive smile, one that shot a sizzling heat to her lower belly and curled her toes.

This guy is so dangerous. And sexy. She tried to keep her mind on asking questions, which, in retrospect, seemed dumb. If she was dreaming, then his answers meant nothing, but it didn't stop her from having an imaginary conversation. "You said something about ingesting memories. I assume you mean Roderick's? How and why would you do that?"

"The how is not important, as to the why, simple. With his memories, even if I don't agree, I can at least understand his actions and find those he's weakened."

"Why would you want to find them? I assure you the asshats he controlled are not worth the effort." Except for maybe Marc. Unlike the leering and creepy guys who hung around Roderick, Marc seemed to have a decent core.

"They might not be the most preferable of companions. However, they must be located because, if they aren't, they will either all die or become slaves to those less benign than I."

There was that dreaded fear again. Like a ball of burning acid, it hurt her chest. "A slave to someone as bad as Roderick?"

"I daresay worse. Roderick might have used you as a peon in his quest to build an army loyal only to him. But my less-compassionate brethren would use you for sick games and torture and to start a war."

It hit her in a moment of clarity. "But they wouldn't go near me if I belonged to you."

"You think me strong enough to protect you?" His lips curved in a mocking grin.

"Aren't you?"

Thaddeus laughed. "Yes. But the better question

is, are you asking me to make you mine? To tie your life to mine until we die? Somehow, I think your wolf might object to that."

"He does." The growled reply preceded Marc's entrance into the cell.

Why did it not surprise her that Marc would also make an appearance in her dream?

She tried to articulate her reasoning. "If I let Thaddeus claim me, then the other vampires can't touch me."

"We barely know the guy, and you'd let him bite you?"

"I barely know you, and yet you expect me to mate with you."

"To protect you."

"Just like I would protect her," Thaddeus added. "I actually think it is a brilliant plan. Albeit, without the wolf. Personally, she could probably survive quite well with just me as her guardian."

"Dream on, bloodsucker." Marc took an aggressive step forward, but before things could escalate, she stepped between them.

"Both of you, stop it. This is a dream. My dream. And that means I'm the one who gets to decide what happens."

"Really?" Thaddeus tossed a wicked smile her way. "Then I should be glad your dream has decided I should kiss you."

"No, it hasn't—" The rest of her rebuttal was swallowed by lips as Thaddeus, in a blur, closed the gap between them and enveloped her in his arms—

and blew all her senses.

Where Marc's kiss was a soft, sensual exploration, Thaddeus undertook a forceful exploration of her mouth. He didn't just conquer her lips; he plundered them.

Where Marc's kiss woke the wolf within her and drew forth a savage need to claim and give as good as she got, Thaddeus evoked a darker sensuality, one that made her want to let him have his way. To have him take charge.

Each different in their style of embrace, yet she couldn't have said which she preferred more. But apparently, they expected her to choose. She found herself spun from the arms of Thaddeus into those of Marc, who feathered kisses across her cheeks and down her neck, each spot he touched tingling with awareness. If wolves could purr, she would have. Instead, she contented herself with gasps and tiny moans of enjoyment.

A blurring motion and she was back in Thaddeus's grasp, his fingers digging into her hips as his tongue invaded her mouth, sliding along hers and causing her to shudder as her arousal rose in pitch.

Not to be outdone, Marc pressed against her back, his soft lips nipping at her nape. Thaddeus sucked on her tongue. Marc blew against the shell of her ear. Their bodies went from clothed to nude in her dream, the heat and hardness of their erections pressing against her, front and back. With her eyes close, she distinguished them by the touch of their hands, the feel of their bodies, and the style of their kiss.

Her body heated. Her arousal spiraled, and she panted. Dream or not, she wanted them, wanted them both. And here, where nothing was truly real, she could do it. Have her vampire lover and the werewolf, too, with no one the wiser. She moaned her assent, and their hands tore at her garments, touching her bare skin and...

She woke suddenly, her skin damp with a sheen of perspiration, the towel lost and the sheets twisted around her bare limbs.

It was just a dream. She could have screamed, especially with her blood still coursing and her arousal pulsing, her clit a throbbing reminder between her legs. Dream or not, she could finish what her imaginary lovers started. She slid her hand down her stomach, over the roundness of it, when a sound halted her. More like a growl in her head.

Aren't I allowed to masturbate?

At first she believed her wolf wanted her to abstain, but it growled again, and this time she caught the intent.

Danger.

The wolf within didn't speak the word so much as think it to her, and Toni took heed. She strained to listen, to hear something out of the ordinary. She even sniffed, but she lacked any true experience to filter what the various scents meant. She could tell some odors belonged to people, staff she assumed who took care of the room. She caught the astringent cleaners used to wipe off the hard surfaces in the room and something fetid, almost rotten, like garbage left out too long, but none seemed out of place in a hotel.

A cold breeze fluttered the curtains and brought a shiver to her skin.

Did someone open the window? She certainly hadn't, and she couldn't imagine Marc doing so. As for the vampire—*my dream lover who claims his name is Thaddeus*—given the alarm clock she faced said four thirty, she highly doubted he was up and about yet, not with the sun still hovering in the sky.

Perhaps the luxury room wasn't properly sealed, or the previous occupant had left the sliding glass door partially ajar.

Or someone had entered via the balcony.

She rolled off the bed a moment before the figure lunged from behind the drapes. She hit the floor with an "Oomph!" The bed springs creaked as her assailant landed on the mattress. Scrabbling on hands and knees, she struggled to move, to cast off the last of her sleep and to get her limbs cooperating.

She didn't make it to her feet before a body hit her in the middle of the back and squashed her flat. Fingers scrabbling at the carpet, she couldn't gain any purchase or buck her attacker off, but she did manage to suck in a lungful of air, which she used to scream, "Help!"

If that hollered plea didn't bring someone running, then she deserved to lose her heroine card because it was perfectly pitched and held just the right note of terror and treble to penetrate even the thickest of hotel-room doors.

A hand gripped her hair roughly and yanked her head back, baring her throat. Fetid breath fluttered against her cheek. "Oh God, no," she sobbed, pinned beneath whatever monster attacked.

The door hit the wall with a *thud* as it slammed open. A russet wolf charged through and soared, hitting the body on her back.

She screamed as the hand tangled in her hair ripped loose, taking strands with it. Flipping over, she gulped for breath through her tears and had a bleary view of the fight. Marc, in his wolf form, snapped and snarled at the vampire who'd attacked them the night before. A vampire who'd returned to finish the job, it seemed. That was disturbing enough, but there was more to make the moment truly horrifying. The truly terrifying part was his neck was obviously still broken, given the way his head tilted at an unnatural angle.

"What goes on here?" Thaddeus appeared in the room, hair rumpled from sleep, wincing as the sliver of sunlight through the gap in the curtains kissed his skin. He stepped back and scowled.

"It's back," she blubbered.

"I see that. Draw our enemy over here," Thaddeus ordered Marc, over here being the shadowy part of the room, where she still cowered on the floor.

She scuttled out of the way as the grappling

bodies rolled toward Thaddeus, whether intentionally or not she couldn't tell. Marc didn't appear to have much luck in clamping his snapping jaws around the rabid vampire. Their foe, on the other hand, seemed more than capable of ripping furrows into Marc's side with dark talons.

It seemed his injury and time spent in the locked trunk had made the vampire even more dangerous.

Thaddeus stepped into the fray, darting in with insane quickness and agility to rip the slavering vampire from Marc. He slammed her attacker against a wall, pinned him there, one hand at its broken throat, the other at his chest. No, in its chest.

Her dark rescuer yanked forth a black beating heart. She gagged and turned away, peering at the happy sunshine spilling through the crack in the drapes. She crawled toward that bright haven, only to yell as something flew overhead, billowing the curtains. The attacking vampire, still twitching even with the gaping hole in his ravaged chest, hit the balcony railing and lay there, in the sun.

Burn, you bastard!

She watched. Waited. It took her a moment to come to a conclusion, a pair of them, actually. One; the fucker wasn't burning. Two; she should have predicted that considering he'd entered via the balcony.

It seemed she wasn't the only one flummoxed by this turn of events. Thaddeus, out of reach of the golden rays, muttered, "Why does he not succumb?"

Marc, who'd returned to his human form, stood

with a wince, the scratches in his side angry and oozing sluggish beads of blood. "Because he's obviously not a fucking vampire."

"Get him back in here before someone notes his existence," Thaddeus ordered.

"If you say so, but you do realize he's not dead."

No, the creature still thrashed, albeit not in any meaningful way. It seemed the loss of its heart had weakened it.

"I'm not an idiot. I can see. But we don't need the authorities banging on the door. We need to figure out what the hell is going on and find a way to dispose of its body."

Toni glanced away as Marc grabbed the creature by a foot and dragged him back in. A black, slimy trail followed it. Feeling her stomach revolt again, Toni scrambled to her feet and bolted for the other room.

She had a feeling she didn't want to see what happened next.

Chapter Seventeen

Thaddeus glanced at the slowing ticking heart in his hand, black with a corrupted stench about it. Even if it had belonged to a vampire, no way would he take a bite. He didn't want power that bad. Striding into the bathroom, he clenched the organ in his fist, squishing it to a pulp. He dropped the remains in the toilet and flushed. Twice. Damned eco-friendly toilets!

The red-haired wolf appeared in the doorway. "I don't think that's going to work for the rest of the body."

Thaddeus snorted. "No, but at least we won't have to worry about the two pieces getting back together."

"You're kidding, right?"

"For once, no. I have no idea what our uninvited guest is capable of."

"What is that thing?"

A question Thaddeus pondered, too. When they'd fought it in the forest, the red gleaming eyes and teeth immediately made him think vampire. Yet, it didn't burn in the sun. It didn't die, even though he'd ripped the heart from it, a sure way, along with decapitation, to kill a vampire. When none of the clues added up, only one conclusion remained. *It's not a vampire.* But if not, then what?

He exited the bathroom, the wolf dancing out of his way before they touched. Hands on his hips, he surveyed the rotten mess on the carpet. "It's not a zombie."

"How can you tell? I mean the thing was dead, or as close to dead as you guys get with a broken neck. I should know. I carried the fucker for a few miles. So how else to explain it coming back to life and not being bothered by sunlight?"

"Zombies don't have beating hearts."

"What does then?"

Something worse. Something forbidden because of the danger. Something Thaddeus hadn't seen in his centuries of life, only heard of. "Ghoul."

"That sounds bad."

"It is. It means we might already be too late. Someone is already gathering the broken wolves set free by Roderick's death. But instead of making them into thralls, or even vampires, they're turning them into ghouls. Half vampires if you will. Creatures that hunger for blood but can withstand sunlight. Monsters that are extremely hard to kill and impossible to control."

"Who the fuck would be crazy enough to do that?"

"I don't know, but I intend to find out." And kill them. The making of ghouls was outlawed for many reasons. The first being the vampire power given to them, the spark needed to make them change, could never be regained. For every ghoul created, the vampire power pool diminished, forever. Secondly, ghouls had one purpose only. Kill and cause mayhem. While they made a formidable fighting force, they were just as likely to turn on their creator as their enemy.

Marc verbalized a startling conclusion just as Thaddeus made the connection. "Hey, if they can't be controlled, then what the fuck was it doing coming after Toni? I mean, we left it locked in a trunk. We're on the ninth fucking floor, and it looks like it came in through the balcony. Why go through all that trouble? Shouldn't it just have escaped when it got the chance?"

"Someone guided its actions." A grim realization.

"But I thought that wasn't possible."

"It's not. I don't understand this any better than you, wolf. But I do know we are no longer safe here. We must dress and depart at once."

"To go where?"

"To find answers, of course."

"What happened to locating the other wolves?"

"We are too few and underpowered to hunt them down, especially if we run into more ghouls. A few we could handle, but if a large number were to swarm us, even I would possibly succumb."

"Can't we call for help?"

He shot the dog a wry glance. "Call whom? Your precious packs, who would laugh to hear that a children's bogeyman is true?"

"What about your vampire friends?"

"Vampires have no friends, just acquaintances who are either trying to bring you down or helping someone else. Never trust them."

"Funny you say that because you expect us to trust you."

"Expect, yes, but it doesn't mean you should." Thaddeus couldn't resist the taunt or the malicious grin. The wolf swallowed hard because of his words, or because Thaddeus had torn the head off the ghoul in the next moment. He couldn't tell, but either way, the Lycan kept him at arm's length.

He left him alone. Just how Thaddeus liked it.

Chapter Eighteen

Toni couldn't help but hear most of the guys' conversation. Apparently a better sense of smell also came with acute hearing. When they emerged from the bedroom, Thaddeus wiping his hands on a white hand towel that would need more than bleach to clean the stains, she was perched on the couch wearing a blanket she'd yanked from the closet.

"Are you okay?" Marc asked.

"If by okay you mean still alive and unhurt, then yes. But I am totally freaked out. Why was that *thing* sent after me?"

She expected Thaddeus to dance around the question or lie. He didn't. "My best guess is it is because you belonged to Roderick. Likely it had orders to either destroy you or bring you back to its master."

On second thought, a little sugarcoating would have been nice. "So, in other words, it could happen again?"

"Not with that particular ghoul, no."

"How can you be sure it's dead this time?"

"Nothing, not even zombies, can survive without a head."

She shuddered, and Marc, seeing it, strode to the couch, in all his naked glory. She averted her gaze but couldn't stop her flaming cheeks.

He ignored her embarrassment and sat beside her, draping an arm across her shoulders. He hugged her close. She couldn't help but recall the dream, a dream where two men hugged her.

Thank God they didn't know about her vivid imagination.

"I'll keep you safe," Marc murmured in her ear. To the vampire, he said, "So where did you want to go to next, Thad?"

Toni started. "Thad? As in short for Thaddeus?"

"Of course," replied Thaddeus. "I thought we cleared that up already."

"But it was a…" She trailed off as her mortified gaze met Thaddeus's grin.

"Dream? Yes, we forged a link while slumbering. One that the wolf joined, probably because of our connection to the late Roderick."

"You mean you were in it, too?" She squeaked the question as she peered at Marc.

He reached a hand and stroked his knuckles along her cheek. "Yes. I was. I told you I felt a connection to you. I just never expected it to run so deep."

"Oh God." She drew up her knees and buried her face in them, cheeks flaming. *I can't believe it really happened, kind of. I hope they don't think we'll be doing it in person.* It was one thing to dream it, another to live it. For one thing, it would probably feel a whole lot more pleasurable.

"I fail to see why you are so embarrassed. You displayed a healthy reaction to a pair of virile males during a time of stress." Thaddeus, with his smooth tone, made it sound so normal. "If we were not pressed for time, I would encourage an exploration of these feelings and encourage you to relieve your sexual tension. However, given the brazenness of this attack, I fear we should make plans to relocate promptly."

"We still don't have clothes though," Marc reminded. "Or were you planning for us to stay in those castoffs looking like your poor cousins?"

"The remedy to your clothing dilemma will arrive at nightfall with Sasha."

A low growl rumbled in Toni's head, and she couldn't help but ask, "Who's Sasha?"

"Sheathe your claws, little wolf. Sasha is a friend of mine, almost like a daughter, you might say. She is also a vampire, which is why she won't arrive until shortly after dusk. I texted her this morning before resting. She will be bringing clothing for both of you, more cash for our travels, as well as sustenance for me."

"You mean blood." Marc boldly stated it.

"Yes, blood. In a bag, if that helps your delicate sensibilities."

"Blood is blood. Drinking it from a bag or a vein, the source is the same."

"True. But it is so much more pleasurable when fresh. I don't suppose you'd care to donate? I'm sure you'd taste delicious."

"Keep your fangs away from me," Marc growled, his body tensing alongside hers.

"Calm yourself. I merely jested. The taking of blood from a vein is an intimate matter, one I prefer to share with my lovers."

Toni tried to ignore the gaze he sent her way. No way was she going to volunteer to feed him, or have sex, no matter how arousing and pleasurable he made it sound.

"What are we going to do about the body?" Marc inclined his head toward the bedroom.

A shudder racked her frame again. *Please don't say we're bringing it with us.*

"The corpse shall be taken care of with none the wiser. Now, if we're done playing the question game, we should ready ourselves for our departure. Nightfall will occur in just over an hour. Seeing as how the bathroom in the guest suite is less than sanitary for the lady, may I offer the use of mine?"

The courtesy surprised her and confused her. One moment, Thaddeus acted the big, bad, murdering vampire with no care for anyone but himself. The next, he did something nice, and unnecessary, throwing her off balance.

"Thank you," she replied. What else could she say? She needed to wash the stench of the ghoul off her, and no way was she chancing that *thing* coming back to life and pulling a *Psycho* moment on her while she bathed.

"I'll stand watch in the bedroom just in case," Marc offered.

"I think your time would be best served cleansing yourself. Unless the body in the bedroom offends your delicate canine sensibilities?"

"I can handle it. But what will you be doing in the meantime?" Marc's query emerged as suspicious—or was the correct term jealous?

"I shall station myself at the desk out here. I need to contact some people. If Antonia will kindly leave the bathroom and bedroom doors slightly ajar, then I can hear should trouble arise and come to her rescue. But," he hastened to add when she gasped, "I doubt that will be necessary. This ghoul only managed to get close because we were careless. It won't happen again."

The words emerged with an ominous ring, and Toni couldn't help but shiver, though not in fear—she had no doubt they'd both prove excellent guards—but in desire. It seemed she harbored a thing for overprotective males.

With time wasting and the sun descending, bringing with it night and who knew what else, Toni hurried to bathe. She needed to cleanse the stench of the ghoul from her hair—as well as rinse the remains of her erotic dream from her skin.

Scooting out from under Marc's arm, she made sure to keep the blanket she'd found tucked snugly around her. Never mind both men had seen the goods. It wasn't her style to run around naked or to try and tempt them into a repeat of her dream.

While her more prudish nature wanted to close and lock the bathroom door, she decided to heed Thaddeus's advice and kept it slightly ajar. She didn't fear anything attacking her in the bathroom. There was no window for an intruder to invade; however, she also wanted to keep an ear on anything happening outside. It seemed caution would become a daily part of her routine, at least for the next little while.

The hot water and steam from the shower did much to soothe her frazzled nerves, but it could do only so much. It didn't quite erase the fear when she'd thought the monster would kill her. It didn't manage to answer the questions and doubts plaguing her, nor ease the sexual tension centered between her legs, but she felt refreshed when all was said and done.

Flipping off the lever to cut the water, she squeaked as she pulled aside the curtain and came face to face with Thaddeus.

"Wh-what are you doing in here?"

"The maid brought up fresh towels. I thought you might like one since I bathed the previous eve."

"Oh. Thank you." She reached out for the fluffy white material, but he had other ideas, instead gesturing for her to step forth from the tub so he could wrap it around her. He even tucked another around her hair.

The gentle attention made her blush, so she kept her gaze averted.

"Sasha has texted me to say she is on her way. The tinted windows in her car give her enough protection to drive and are well worth the occasional ticket we get from the local authorities about them not being legal."

"Why doesn't she just whammy them into letting her off scot-free?" she asked as she followed him out to the main bedroom area.

"Sasha's powers of persuasion aren't as refined as mine. Her strengths lie in other areas."

"And what's your power?"

Staring at his back, she wasn't prepared for the amused glance he shot over his shoulder. It tickled the simmering heat she kept trying to ignore.

"Trying to get me to spill my secrets?" he asked.

"No. Just making small talk."

"Ah yes, meaningless conversation, a means of flirting and getting to know a potential lover."

Why, of all the presumptuous things! "That's not what I was doing. And we're not going to be lovers. That dream was an aberration. It won't happen again."

He arched a brow. "I didn't take you for a liar."

She usually wasn't. She angled her chin. "You don't know anything about me."

"I know more than you think." One moment he stood by the bed, and the next, he was before her, standing close, too close. "There is something between us, little wolf."

"Yeah, a towel, and it's not coming off."

"Ever ready with a comeback. An interesting quirk you have, diffusing situations where you're not completely in control."

"I'm in perfect control."

"Really? And yet your heart is racing, the temperature of your body rising. I'll even wager were

I to touch you, intimately, that your honey would kiss my fingertips."

How did he know? "You wish."

"I know. I feel…" He lowered his voice. "And I want."

He titled her chin with a finger, and she couldn't help but get sucked into his dark gaze, but unlike before, she retained all her wits. Her body was her own. She could have moved away. So what excuse did she have for letting him kiss her?

And enjoying it.

Chapter Nineteen

Marc didn't mean to spend too much time in the shower, but once he got under the hot spray, he couldn't help but enjoy it. The dirt accumulated over days of running through the woods, plus a few battles, sloughed from his skin, leaving him refreshed. In body, at least. His mind though, that was another matter.

What happened?

And he wasn't referring to the ghoul or even the events in the woods that led to his meeting Thad, the annoying vampire. He was more curious about the dream, the dream he'd shared with Toni. A dream where he shared Toni with Thad.

A connection existed between him and the she-wolf, of that he was certain. The more time he spent with her, the more he wanted to claim her. Hell, the only reason he hadn't given in to his wolf's frenzied demand was because taking Toni by force would only push her away—and give root to the kernel of evil he feared nestled within him.

I won't fuck this up.

Something he'd overhead in the dream before interrupting, something both Thad and Thea had said about ingesting memories, struck a chord with Marc. He couldn't help but recall his inhalation of Roderick's ashes. Ashes he was pretty certain

Thaddeus carried in his trunk. Which begged the question, why?

Why would anyone want the remains of a sick vampire?

Why, to partake of the passed one's power, of course.

Where this ghostly knowledge or certainty came from he wasn't sure, but if he had to wager a guess, he'd say Roderick or, rather, the memories Roderick carried. Ghostly remembrances, events seen through a different set of eyes and corrupted ideals, all that and more flitted through Marc's brain, making him doubt his sanity. Making him fear for his mind…and his soul.

Given he couldn't truly be sure his actions were his own, was it any wonder he held off on marking Antonia? Even if Pack law gave him every right to claim a she-wolf without a guardian, was he truly the best choice for her?

Besides, why force it when his gut said she'd come to him on her own? He couldn't forget how she'd melted in his arms and thoroughly enjoyed their kiss. He couldn't stop reliving the moment in the dream, the embrace. And not just the one of the lips but also the body-to-body one where he'd pressed against her back and Thad pressed from the front, cocooning their woman in protection. Pleasuring her, both at once as Pack lore dictated.

Except Thad wasn't pack. He was a vampire, and Marc was nuts to even think of sharing a woman, any woman, with a two-timing backstabbing bloodsucker.

Or was he? Thad hadn't done anything yet to earn distrust. On the contrary, the asshole had saved their lives, come to their rescue, and provided help even though he could have walked away. Hell, he could have fled with Toni, leaving Marc in his dust, and yet Thad hadn't. Marc wasn't an idiot. He knew the vampire was more powerful than him, but Thad treated Marc if not like an equal than as a close second—and, given his mocking insults, almost like a friend.

Gasp! Could it be they could consider themselves partners in whatever events conspired against them?

Vampire or not, Thad wasn't the true enemy, and for the moment, Marc needed him as an ally.

Until I can rejoin the pack.

Now there was a whole other dilemma. Somehow, the idea of placing himself under someone's watchful and distrustful eye, subject to their stringent rules, didn't appeal. Yet he expected Toni to.

No wonder she's balking. If a guy raised to obey doesn't want to cave to their laws, then how can I expect her to just toss away her life and dreams to follow them?

Yet what other choice was there? Being an outcast was a lonely life. *However, if Toni and I mated, we'd have each other.*

Dangerous thoughts, yet he couldn't help mulling them over. Muddling through the turmoil in his mind kept him in the shower longer than expected. He stepped from the stall and wrapped a towel around his hips, and the cooler air of the room felt refreshing on his feverish skin. As he toweled his hair with brisk strokes, it hit him. The silence in the hotel suite struck him as too loud. What was the vampire up to?

He strode out into the main area, and surprise! Thad wasn't at his post, but his things were.

Son of a bitch. He's making a move on my woman.

Keeping his temper in hand meant he didn't run, but Marc didn't waste time either entering the other bedroom then stopping. A myriad of emotions assailed him, first and foremost an inner growl from his wolf at the sight before them.

Thad was locked in an embrace with Toni, and not an unwilling one judging by her soft sounds of pleasure and the way she had her arms draped around his neck. Her damp towel hung loosely, caught between their bodies, the dangling fabric showcasing the roundness of her ass.

As if reliving the dream, Marc approached them, his bare feet making no sound in the plush carpet. He stopped just behind her, hesitant, but not out of jealousy. On the contrary, arousal beset him.

A part of him wondered that he didn't yank the vampire away, a vampire he knew was aware of his presence. Yet, that jealous action seemed out of place when faced with the sensuous nature of the embrace. An embrace he wanted a part of.

The light kiss he placed on her nape didn't startle Toni, but a shiver did run through her frame.

Encouraged, Marc stepped closer, letting his

towel drop, placing his still-damp body against her back. His engorged cock pressed hot and hard against her plush backside, and he heard her suck in a breath.

To his surprise, the vampire did not motion him away or attempt to keep her to himself. On the contrary, male fingers grasped his hips and pulled him tighter against her, encouraging him to grind.

Oh yes. Marc sucked at the tender skin of her neck, working his way up to her earlobe. He nipped the flesh, tugging at it while rubbing his dick up and down the crease of her buttocks. Thad abandoned her mouth to kiss his way down the front of her, stopping to lavish attention on her breasts, her full and succulent breasts.

As a spectator, Marc enjoyed a feast of his own. His mouth watered, but he'd have to wait his turn for a taste of those berries. Feathering his lips along her jaw, his subtle caresses had her head tilting back and sideways until he could feast upon her mouth, her tongue not shy at all as it darted out to dance with his. A soft moan escaped her. Marc groaned in reply.

Someone cleared their throat and, clearly amused, said, "Thank goodness I'm not a ghoul, or I'd be eating a sandwich right now."

Chapter Twenty

As interruptions went, this had to rank as one of the worst. Thaddeus raised his head and glared at Sasha over Toni's shoulder. "Would it kill you to knock?"

Sasha shrugged, completely unapologetic. "Sorry, boss. You know me."

Indeed he did. What Sasha lacked in ability to compel, she made up for in minor magic, namely the unlocking of locks and the movement of objects. Telekinesis in other words. And sneakiness. The girl could sneak into anywhere without raising suspicion.

Still, gifts or not, rudeness was inexcusable, and he'd have to talk to his adopted daughter later about boundaries, especially if Toni were to become a regular part of his life, if she ever forgave him for the embarrassment that had her blushing bright.

It didn't take reading her thoughts to see she regretted getting caught. He'd have to teach her to shutter her emotions if she didn't want people to use them against her. Another thing to address later. Right now, they had pressing business to take care. Besides, a part of him wanted to enjoy her delightfully innocent response to embarrassment for a while longer.

While he—and the damnable wolf he couldn't seem to shake—pleasured the delightful Antonia, night had fallen. With night came a whole new set of predators and possible dangers. It made his transformed heart beat a little faster and his blood flow quickly at the thought of the possible excitement awaiting him.

Nothing like the anticipation of violence and death to get a vampire's adrenaline going.

Dropping a light kiss on Antonia's forehead, he murmured, "We shall finish this later."

He ignored her muttered, "Or not."

The she-wolf could deny or protest all she wanted, but the truth was she desired him. Unfortunately that desire seemed to include the male wolf as well. Lucky for Marc, however, Thaddeus had taken time to ponder their unusual situation and had concluded that sharing might be a good thing.

With female wolves being somewhat rare, and pack laws so stringent, or so he understood, it wouldn't hurt to have Antonia tied to a male wolf. One with no loyalty to any pack. One he could hopefully convince to follow his rule.

The fact that Thaddeus was even considering allowing not one but two wolves into his carefully ordered life should have sent him on a killing rampage and fleeing for his nearest solitary retreat. It didn't. Good news was, if that changed, he could always give in to his murderous impulses, or order Sasha to do it. The girl really had no conscience. One of the things he admired most about her, that and her loyalty to him.

"Have you brought what I asked?" he demanded, leaving Antonia to Marc's care as he led

Sasha from the room.

"I did. Clothes for them both, weapons, and your grimoire, which, I might add, you could have accessed via your phone."

Thaddeus made a face. "I don't like the scanned version. It lacks a certain something."

"Yeah, dust mites and paper cuts."

No, it went deeper than that. The grimoire itself didn't just retell vampire lore and itemize things of magic, including creatures and other things; it was *magic*. Whether some long-ago spell caster imbued it, or the book itself soaked up residual power like a sponge, something about it was different. Special. Necessary to his methods. Leafing through its pages helped Thaddeus hone his intuition and often focus his jumbled thoughts. "Not everything needs to be high tech," he told his protégé, not for the first time.

"Whatever, old man. So now that I'm here, mind telling me what the heck is going on?"

"I thought I elucidated myself in the text I sent you."

Sasha rolled her eyes. "Oh, because that was so helpful. The one you sent this morning was, 'Killed unknown fledgling. Acquired two wolves. Need clothing for female and male. Bring ASAP.'"

"You know how I dislike relaying too much via text. Anyone can read them."

"I know, oh paranoid one. Big brother is watching, blah, blah, blah. But seriously, how do you expect me to figure shit out? I mean, look at the one you sent after you got up. 'Ghoul attack. Need book and weapons.'"

What more did she need? A video? "Excellent, so you are up to date."

Biting back a grin, Thaddeus kept a smooth expression as Sasha stared at him. "You call that up to date? How about, why the hell did you keep those wolves, other than the obvious that you have a thing for the girl? What about what the fuck happened with the council? You do know Morpheus has put a bounty on your head, a big one. Every vampire and his army of minions will be after you now."

"How much?"

"Does it matter?"

"Just curious. The last bounty on my head was for a chest full of gold coins, but of course, that was quite some time ago."

"Five million."

He frowned. "So little? My death is worth at least ten times that."

"Nice to see the size of your ego hasn't changed."

Why pretend false modesty? Thaddeus was well aware of his own worth. "What reason did he give for my termination?"

"None, but the prevailing rumor is you two are fighting over who controls the council."

"Technically, Morpheus is in charge for the moment, given the other members are his sycophants. But they don't matter. Everyone knows they are but figureheads. What about the other factions? Can I expect support against him?"

"Honestly? Not really. You haven't exactly endeared yourself to our community, what with your lack of patience in idiots resulting in your killing a bunch of them. But then again, for every vampire that hates you, two more abhor Morpheus. I think the majority are planning to hunker down, watch, and wait for the pair of you to destroy each other."

Not exactly the best of news, but not completely unexpected. Actually, this could work in his favor. If none sided with Morpheus, then that meant few would know of his plans or the revelations of what Roderick's wolves could mean. Perhaps Thaddeus could still avert a war with the Lycans with no one the wiser.

"Who are you wagering on?" he asked.

She grinned. "You, of course, boss. I'm not so stupid as to underestimate you, especially not when you get that look in your eye."

"What look?"

"The one that says 'bring it, asshole.'"

He laughed. "Do I seem that eager?" She arched a brow, and he laughed again. "Yes, I guess I am. It's been a while since I've engaged in such excitement."

"Is that why you're knocking boots with two wolves? That seems a little wild, even for you."

He shrugged. "What can I say? The woman appeals, but unfortunately, she comes already partially claimed."

"Since when do you share?"

He didn't, yet with the changing times and the situation, he was open-minded enough to see where it went. "Forget my love life. How come you're not questioning me about the ghoul?"

"Because I assumed it was auto-correct. Do you mean to say you actually encountered one? I thought those things were just a legend."

"So did I, but the body in the other room is proof otherwise."

"Any idea who sent it?"

He shrugged. "I never had a chance to question it or really conduct any investigation. Things happened too fast."

"In other words, you killed it instead of containing it." She shook her head as if scolding him.

"The thing was rabid. I needed to do something."

"You did something all right. You killed your only clue to its creator."

An urge to throttle his protégé raised its head. Thaddeus resisted. He deserved the dressing down. He'd acted rashly. They'd not been in true danger, so he could have handled the situation differently, yet something about Toni's fear struck a chord in him. He didn't like to see it, so he'd dealt with the source. All internal truths he didn't relay out loud. Again, the whole reputation thing, not to mention the mocking. Sasha would never let him live it down. "I want you to take a look in the other room. Tell me if you recognize the body."

Sasha left and quickly returned, shaking her head. "Never seen him before."

"So we still don't know if he's a puppet of Morpheus's or if there's another player. A shame. We could have used that against him to further split the factions."

"What are you planning to do with the body? You can't exactly leave it for the authorities to find."

"I've got a plan. First, though, I'm going to need the clothes you brought. I've left a certain pair of wolves in the nude alone long enough." And while he could sense them straining to listen, and not cavorting naked upon his sheets, no need to keep temptation on display. He had other fires to light.

Chapter Twenty-One

Toni gaped at the top floor of the hotel, at what she could see through the billowing black smoke and occasional licking flames shooting from the shattered windows.

"You set the room on fire." She still couldn't believe it. When Thaddeus had hurried them out of the suite, she'd wondered at his haste. Did he fear another attack? Were the authorities on their way, alerted by other guests of the strange goings on?

Not exactly. It turned out her vampire was a bit of a pyro.

"We couldn't leave evidence behind, namely traces of DNA or the ghoul. There is only one sure way to erase it."

"But the other guests…" She waved her hands.

"Will be fine, I'm sure. Maybe a little smoke inhalation and hysterics, but this place was built out of cement and steel. It helps contain fiery mishaps so that they don't completely destroy the structure."

"I'm sure that's a relief to them," Marc added, his sarcasm evident.

The newest member of their group, Sasha, grinned. "If you think this is bad, then wait until you really get to know him."

"Sasha." Thaddeus's voice held a warning tone, which she ignored.

"You should see what he does to people who really piss him off.

"Don't you have some tasks to attend to?" Thaddeus stared at her, but she didn't cower or flinch, a fact Toni found interesting. Big, bad, murderous and property-destroying badass, and yet, Thaddeus was obviously well loved by the playful vampire who'd arrived with some much-needed clothing.

Sasha snapped a hand to her forehead in a salute. "Aye, aye, Captain. I shall gather the troops and scurry off to do thy bidding ASAP."

"What tasks?" Marc asked.

"Nefarious ones, of course," Sasha replied with a wink. "It's what we vampires excel at."

Sliding into a sleek red convertible, a Mustang by the logo, with an engine that growled, Sasha left in a squeal of tires and blaring music.

Marc shook his head. "Is it just me, or does she seem like your total opposite, Thad?"

A bemused look on his face, Thaddeus replied, "Sasha is special. Sometimes a little too lighthearted, but despite her jests, she's loyal. We can trust her with our lives."

Toni had to wonder, given his tone, just how many people he could truly say that about with confidence. "Where is she going?"

"She, some other thralls, and vampires are going to see what they can do about rounding up more of Roderick's stray wolves."

"I thought it was too dangerous."

"If unprepared. I assure you, Sasha has enough backup, both in bodies and firepower, to take care of anything they might find."

"How are they going to find the rogues?"

"Tracking via old-fashioned methods, a bit of magic, checking out the areas surrounding known Roderick hideouts. The saner ones will have managed to leave the woods and seek out food and shelter. The damaged ones won't be concerned about covering their trails."

"Are they going to kill them?" Marc asked.

Gesturing to the car, Thaddeus waited until they'd slid into the backseat before replying. "They've got orders to defend themselves."

"From wolves who will take one whiff and automatically think they're the enemy."

"Do you have a better plan? I applied for help from the nearest Pack. Their leader, Nathan, has declined to provide support. When I warned him of a possible war and attack by Morpheus and his army, he decided it was best if the Lycans stayed within the compound."

"Makes sense. They can't leave the women and children undefended."

Rescue came from an unlikely source. "What century are you from? I'd expect that kind of chauvinism from Thad, but not you. I mean, come on, give us a little credit. Women aren't entirely helpless. We might not be as big or trained when it comes to fighting, but even the tiniest woman can handle a gun," Toni pointed out. "I'd think helping their kind would have some kind of priority."

Marc came to the Pack's defense. "You're talking about putting sane and healthy wolves on the trail of possibly murderous ones. Why risk their lives? I can see Nathan's point. Even if he did capture some, what would they do with them? Where could they keep them? In a sense, so long as the crazy rogues are not attacking humans, isn't it better to let them roam wild until Mother Nature takes her course? From the sounds of it, many of these wolves won't have the skills or mindset to survive the coming winter."

"Yet doesn't leaving them free mean those wolves could get compelled by this Morpheus guy if he does take the time to locate them?" Toni pointed out.

"Excellent observation, little wolf. That is exactly why I've sent Sasha to see if she can find them first. Alas, I fear we're already running late. The ghoul we located was probably one of them. And despite the difficulty in making and controlling them, I'd wager part of my fortune that there are others."

"Can Sasha and your guys handle them?"

"So long as they're not attacked en masse, yes."

A prospect she could tell bothered him, yet oddly enough, it wasn't his face or tone that gave him away, more a burst of emotion that she felt. How strange. "What about the wolves they find? You say they're supposed to gather them, to do what?" If Marc's Pack was unwilling to take them in, then what would Thaddeus do to them?

"I've got a ranch a few hours from here she can bring the tainted Lycans to. Once there, we can decide what to do with them."

"Will you let them return to their packs?" Marc tensed beside her, waiting for an answer.

Halted at a red light, Thaddeus drummed his fingers on the steering wheel. "I don't know."

"What do you mean you don't know? What do you plan to do with them?"

"I think that would depend on their state of mind. You and I both know the crazy ones can't be allowed to reveal our secrets."

"I can see the need to imprison those, but what of the others, the ones who did regain their minds?"

Thaddeus danced around the question. "This is a very delicate situation. One never seen before."

"And? These wolves, those people, never asked to get fucked over by Roderick. If we find them, why shouldn't they get a second chance?"

"Why do they deserve one?" Thaddeus fired back.

Marc flinched beside her, and Toni put a hand on his arm. "Because they were victims," she said, her voice soft. "Like me and Marc. Is this your way of saying we're stuck with whatever decision you make about our future?"

"Marc is a special case. Whatever happened between him and Roderick didn't leave him susceptible to mind tricks. Being able to resist them means I don't have to worry about someone using him as a pawn. Although they still might try to kill him." Thaddeus just couldn't resist saying it with a gleeful tone and smile. "He's also seemingly sane, if one discounts the fact he's partnered with a vampire."

The jest fell flat. "So Marc's safe. Great. What about me?" she asked. "I'm not broken, but it seems any vampire can compel me, which makes me a risk. What will happen to me?"

"We both know the answer to that."

She slumped. "So kudos for me I didn't go crazy, but boo for me, my free will is up for grabs. Does that mean I get to be your prisoner forever?"

"I prefer the term lover. As my mistress, you will have a link to me that will protect you."

His eyes promised her delight, and he'd probably stay true to his promise, but what about in a few years? Would she come to resent him for deciding her future?

"What are her other options?" Marc demanded.

"Death." Flatly said.

"Excuse me?" she squeaked.

Thaddeus met her gaze in the rearview mirror. "Much as I am intrigued by you, self-preservation comes first. You wandering about unclaimed poses a danger not only to me through our association but the whole vampire and even Lycan community. You know too much. You are a weakness waiting for someone to exploit. If you find the thought of being my lover so abhorrent, then I can either find you another vampire master, or you can always choose the martyred route of death."

"Or you can give her the same immunity I have," Marc declared.

The car swerved before slamming to a stop, jolting them. Not far, though, because this time, forewarned about his insane driving, she'd actually buckled up.

Thaddeus craned around in the driver seat to direct an intent stare at Marc. "What do you mean give her the same immunity? Explain yourself, wolf."

"I think I know why you can't compel me, why we're linked, and I think it has to do with Roderick's ashes."

"What do you know of those?" Thaddeus demanded.

"Before some dude arrived in a limo to scoop them up, I breathed some in. Swallowed some, too, when I sneezed. It's done something to me. I get weird glimpses of shit I shouldn't know. Roderick things. And I'm pretty sure they're the reason why, despite the fact I was one of his rogues, I'm immune to vampires."

"I've never heard of a thrall gaining immunity before. However, your ingestion of them would explain a lot," muttered Thaddeus.

"So I'm right, then?" Marc pressed. "The ashes have power, don't they?"

"Perhaps." Thaddeus turned away, but Marc wouldn't let the revelation rest.

"Stop it with the cryptic shit. Will they or won't they protect Toni from being compelled?"

"If what you say is true, then, yes, possibly. But we don't know that for sure."

"We could try."

"We could hold on a second, too," Toni interjected. "Or has it not occurred to you freaks that you're asking me to snort—"

"Or eat," Thaddeus supplied, unhelpfully.

"The ashes of a dead vampire. Am I the only one who thinks that's fucking gross?"

"It's not so bad."

"You mean you've done it?"

Again, Thaddeus caught her gaze in the mirror. "How do you think I found you? How do you think Sasha is tracking the others?"

She swallowed the sour panic in her mouth. "You mean you've all eaten ashes. Marc, I can understand, you sniffed them as your wolf, it was accidental, but why would you intentionally do that? Even to track us. I mean, that's crazy. Nasty. Not to mention, we're talking Roderick here. Why would anyone want something of that monster in them?"

Thaddeus didn't reply for a long time. She could almost see the gears of his mind whirring as he debated how much to tell them. How much to hide.

"What I say is never to be revealed. I am about to tell you one of the biggest secrets of vampires."

"Is this where you make us do a pinkie oath and swear to kill us if we break it?" Marc mocked his serious tone.

"Don't push me, dog. I've already told you too much, and you seem to forget, I have no conscience when it comes to killing. I'm already damned, so what's one more death?" Thaddeus grinned over his shoulder, his pointed canines glinting in the passing car headlights.

"No need to kill anyone. We promise not to tell," Toni vowed. When Marc didn't follow suit, she elbowed him.

"Fine. I promise not to tell. Besides, who would believe me?"

"First you need to know a certain basic fact about the creation of vampires, or vampires in general. We will never multiply or overrun humanity like so many books and movies fear. You see, our power is finite."

"Which means?" Marc queried.

"There is only so much vampire essence in the world. Each time we create a new vampire, the creator loses part of his or her essence. The amount depends on how much they are willing to give to their creation."

"So you need to donate your vampire shit to make a vampire."

"Put simply, yes."

"Good to know, but it doesn't explain the ashes."

"Doesn't it? Think of it. Since there is only a finite pool, each time a vampire dies, that essence should be lost. Over time, we would become extinct."

"Unless you reabsorb it." Toni began to see where this was going, and it wasn't pleasant.

"When one of my kind is terminated, in order to bring his or her power back into the fold, ingestion of the remains is required. Which I know makes little sense. You'd figure their power would release upon the world and just rejoin the source, but it doesn't. We need to eat, absorb, snort, inject...You get the picture. The method isn't important, just the actual absorption."

"Is that why you're so strong?" Toni asked. "Because you've"—*ugh*—"eaten your enemies?"

"And shared very little of it." Thaddeus nodded. "I've got quite the name for myself in our community. In my early days, when I was struggling to make my mark and set myself as a force to be reckoned with, I ambushed and killed a lot of my kind. Back then, some of the masters were more willing to share their power to have an army of vampires they could call their own. But the power of one split among so many makes for weak creations. I swept through them like a dark tide, ripping out hearts and devouring them as they still beat. You get the bulk of the vampire's strength like that. The rest of the body only holds weak remnants."

Marc made a face, an expression she surely mirrored. "Dude, that is fucking gross. And this is from a guy who chases squirrels and eats them."

"As I said, that was a long time ago. I've since given up my more carnivorous pursuits. I discovered that even cooked or, in some cases, ashed, I can still absorb the essence."

Toni couldn't help saying, "But you still eat

them. Doesn't that make you a cannibal?"

"I prefer the term carnivore. Dead meat is dead meat. I'm not saying it makes the most appetizing of meals, but it's necessary if the essence isn't to go to waste."

"But you're already so strong now. Why keep eating? Couldn't you just bury him? Don't you have enough power?" Toni tried to reconcile the ardent lover with the unrepentant cannibal. It was hard. On the one hand, his dark side repulsed her. His very nature disgusted her. Yet, outwardly he remained the same: handsome, engaging, and still her only viable choice aside from Marc.

"Burying Roderick's ashes, or any other vampires, means giving the essence to someone else, possibly my enemy."

Marc grabbed her hand and squeezed it. "I think we need to get off the topic of body eating and back to the consequences. You say you have Roderick's ashes and that they led you to us. How?"

"It is not just vampiric essence that gets reabsorbed. In some cases, we also recall some of the memories, sometimes even the personality of the previous owner. And even rarer, those that the vampire ingested in his lifetime. Sometimes we can also reestablish an esoteric link of a sort with the thralls in their power."

"That's insane!" she exclaimed.

"Indeed. Madness lurks for those not careful. It is why most vampires choose to share the bodies of our foes, lest too much of a single entity blur the lines of our own mind. It is why I only partook of some of Roderick's ashes. The remainder I've shared with Sasha and a few of my trusted minions."

"So there's none left?" Marc questioned, his tone perturbed.

"I didn't say that. There is some. Not a great deal, but enough to attempt what you are suggesting."

"What if I don't want to eat dead Roderick?" she asked.

"Then choose, little wolf. Vampire lover, thrall, or death?"

Chapter Twenty-Two

Marc couldn't blame Toni for her hesitation. Look at them, standing on the side of the road, the ornate box of ashes sitting on the hood, lid open waiting for Toni to act. He could smell the char and, worse, knew what it was from.

At least when he'd snorted them, he'd done so accidentally, never realizing what it meant. But then again, if someone would have told him that the ashes would make him immune to the compulsion of vampires? He probably would have swallowed more just to be sure.

Thaddeus wisely didn't push the matter, allowing Toni to decide for herself, even if her decision options weren't exactly great. Become a vampire's sex slave—dressing it up as lover didn't make it any prettier—death, or sucking back some barbecued vampire.

She made the only real choice.

Toni ducked her head and inhaled. Coughed. Choked. Sucked in some more nasty dust and reeled back. Thaddeus was quick to slap down the lid on the box before too much of the depleted ash could escape. Still a few drifting motes danced on the light breeze.

Marc ignored them and Thad in favor of placing an arm around Toni, whose eyes watered as she gagged.

"Gross. Ick. Nasty," she ranted, pausing only to chug back an entire water bottle that Thaddeus handed her.

Only once she'd rinsed her mouth and palate did she glare at their vampire companion. "Okay, let's see if you guys were right or if I just snorted a dead guy for nothing."

Thaddeus stepped closer, his dark gaze boring into hers. His voice emerged as a slow, seductive whisper. "You want to kiss me. Lick the seam of my lips before tonguing me and wrapping your arms around my body. You want me to make love to you, to have me drape you over the hood of this car and penetrate your lush body."

Toni did no such thing. She blinked. "Are you done being a perv?"

"I take it you feel no compulsion to rip my clothes off and have your wicked way with me?"

A taunting smile curved her lips. "Oh, I do, not because you told me to, but because you're a hot bastard. But that I can ignore."

A twinge of jealousy made Marc's wolf growl inside, but not for long. She turned a beaming smile his way. "It worked. I don't have to be any vampire's slave."

"Yay," Thaddeus cheered in the driest tone imaginable.

"You sound disappointed, bloodsucker," Marc taunted.

"I am. I can't deny I looked forward to a lifetime

pampering you, little wolf. But the delightful outcome to this experiment is that now, when you do come to me, you won't be able to claim it's because of my power. When we do become lovers, it will be because you recognize the desire we have for each other is real and true."

Marc waited for her to shut the vampire down, to tell him in no uncertain terms it would never happen.

Instead, she asked him a question. "Why? Why are you so interested in me? And don't give me some bullshit about my being the hottest woman you've ever met or any other crap. What do you see in me that you think is so special?"

"When you've lived as long as I have, you understand all too soon that the exterior of a person is fleeting. Looks fade. Youth passes in a flash. When choosing a long-term companion, I prefer to judge on what a person has inside."

"And what do you see in me?"

"Strength. Courage. A spirit to live and an unwillingness to let the past drag her down. I see someone who would be loyal. Loving. Supportive. Someone who won't let others push her around."

"You can tell all that from just a few days?"

"Don't forget I've had access to your thoughts, emotions, and even some of your memories. I know you better than you probably know yourself."

"Did you also see that I can be bitchy sometimes for no reason other than I hate rainy days? That my ex-boyfriends complained I didn't have a high enough sex drive and that I like to binge eat junk food while watching every episode of *Supernatural?*"

Marc, watching their byplay, couldn't help but feel a little left out but fascinated. While he didn't get the same chance to sift through her memories, he'd noticed some of the same attributes that drew Thad. It seemed she attracted them both just by being her. *And it doesn't hurt that she comes in a hot package.*

"I want you as you are, little wolf."

Her lips parted on a sigh. "For a really old guy, you do know how to sweet talk to a girl. But"—she shook her head—"pretty words don't mean I'm going to jump into bed with you. Not to mention, I've also got this whole wolf thing to deal with." Her fingers curled around Marc's. "As attracted as I am to you, I am also drawn to Marc. It's the oddest thing. I feel like I have a connection to both of you, and I'm having a hard time figuring out if it's because of the whole Roderick thing or something else."

Marc brushed his thumb over the back of her hand. "Some of our stories talk about the mating urge. Most scoff at it, but your words remind me of it. We have legends we've passed down, treat like fairy tales, of men and women who are destined to be together, who feel an uncontrollable passion and need for one another."

Thaddeus snorted. "Not that mating thing again. Didn't we get enough of that with *Twilight?*"

"Hey," Toni interjected. "I happened to like that

movie."

Marc didn't because, in the end, the vampire got the girl.

Chapter Twenty-Three

After that odd, yet intense conversation, they got back on the road, to where Thaddeus wouldn't say, which, of course ,drove Marc nuts.

"Why are you being so closemouthed?"

"The less you know, the less you can tell my enemies."

"Are you sure you don't want to blindfold us then?" was Marc's sarcastic retort.

"Not necessary, although I am seriously thinking about duct taping your mouth shut."

To the sound of their bickering, Toni, exhausted by recent events, slept, her head pillowed in Marc's lap, his hand lightly stroking her hair from her face as he continued to bait the vampire.

It was crazy how comforted she felt in his presence. How safe. Don't get her wrong, she still had a thing for Marc, which made it initially too sensitive for her to lie across his legs, but she tamped down her interest and let the drone of the car engine and Marc's soothing touch, not to mention the oddly reassuring sound of both men bantering, put her to sleep.

A dreamless one this time. A shame.

What seemed like only minutes later, a gentle shake and a murmured, "Toni, time to wake up," saw her stretching with a wide yawn, only to freeze when she opened her eyes.

She'd forgotten where she napped. She remembered right quick when she noted her open mouth was less than an inch away from Marc's groin, a groin that increased in size the longer she stared.

Heat rising in her cheeks, she scrambled to a seated position and shot Marc a glance. His blue eyes danced with mirth. "Hi."

"Hi. Thanks for letting me use you as a pillow, and sorry if I drooled."

"I didn't mind. You can *use* me anytime you like, for *anything* you want."

Somehow she suspected he didn't mean as a cushion for her head.

The passenger door opened, and Thaddeus offered her a hand. She eschewed it and clambered out on her own, stretching out the kinks in her body from her contorted nap in the backseat.

"Where are we?" she asked as she took in their locale. A gravel driveway lined with a wild profusion of plants, the leaves and flowers still in bloom despite the fall weather. A ranch-style home covered in weathered cedar shingles sat before them, all the windows dark but one.

"We're visiting an old friend of mine," was Thaddeus's unhelpful reply.

"Isn't it kind of late to pop in?"

"People who are friends with vampires are used to our nocturnal hours. Fear not, she will welcome us."

She?

Toni couldn't help but bristle, and as if sensing her jealous spurt, Thaddeus laughed.

"You have nothing to fear, little wolf. You are the only one to pique my interest. Come. She awaits us."

Ominous sounding, kind of like the location. Middle of nowhere, surrounded by trees. Then, smack-dab in the middle of a yard, bordered by purple mums and evergreens, a house.

Innocuous as it seemed, Toni couldn't help her frisson of fear. Maybe it had to do with the stillness bereft of normal night sounds. Perhaps it was the fact they were who knew where without even the reassuring sound of traffic or neighborhood streetlights. Whatever the reason for her unease, Toni didn't shrug aside the fingers Marc laced through hers, or step away from the hand Thaddeus placed in the small of her back. On the contrary, she welcomed their unique touch and support. Positioned between them, she felt safe.

The walkway, the unkept cracks filled with lichen, was strewn with fallen leaves that crunched as they stepped on them. The front stoop consisted of a cement step and poured slab porch, the faded welcome mat reminding visitors to wipe their feet. The door to the home was intriguing. Made of wood, someone had taken the time to carve, in intricate detail, images and symbols.

While Thaddeus rapped on it sharply, three times, she took closer note of the handiwork, in particular the disturbing birds with overly large wings and teeth. Lifelike and savage looking. She was thankful they weren't real but wondered what kind of disturbed mind would create them. She also tried to make sense of the symbols strewn over the surface. They almost seemed to shift and move the more she stared. Maybe if she placed her hand on one to—

The door opened all of a sudden, without a creak or warning, or anybody there for that matter. Screw what the mat said. Within, the house appeared dark and definitely not welcoming. Inside her head, her wolf whined, and it didn't take Dr. Dolittle to decipher her message that this place held danger. No shit. But where could she go? Her escorts seemed determined to visit the broad who lived here.

Thaddeus prodded her forward, but she held back. "Are you sure we should go in?"

"We are invited."

By who, Casper the resident ghost?

Marc didn't seem to have a problem. He stepped over the threshold, and since he still held her hand, she followed with Thaddeus covering the rear.

The door slammed shut, leaving them momentarily in darkness. She couldn't help but tighten her grip on Marc's hand, especially when candles flickered to life within amber glass sconces on the wall.

I think I preferred the dark. At least in the dark she could have pretended they'd entered a normal home.

In the dancing candlelight, she noticed they

stood in a large front hall, much larger than the house indicated, especially since the ceiling soared at least two stories overhead, which made no sense. From the outside, there was only one level.

What kind of fucked-up illusion is this? She sidled closer to Thad while keeping her death grip on Marc. Hedging her bets and playing the part of maiden in need of protection? Fucking right. While she wasn't afraid to fight, it didn't hurt to have the solid protection of two males.

"Where are we?" Marc asked, not seemingly bothered at all, or was it an act? If her wolf was going batty in her head, whining they should get out, what was his doing?

She envied his composure, especially when faced with the weirdness around them. Take, for example, the wallpaper seemingly comprised of screaming ghostly faces. At least those she could have chalked to poor interior design. Ditto for the mounted ornaments, animal heads in most cases, deer, moose, wolf—*grrrr*—lion. Was this woman some kind of hunter? Did Thaddeus hope to engage her services?

The most important question being, how does this woman feel about werewolves? She'd hate for her or Marc's head to adorn these walls. A few more steps in and she felt as if they'd stepped into another dimension, as among the normal coterie of animals she also spotted more humanlike trophies, but humans like she'd never seen. For example, the one with porcine features including snout and tusks. There was a scaly-skinned face with no nose, just slits between the mouth and eyes. Oh, and then there was the pièce de résistance, the object that caught her stare, the horse head with the gleaming spire jutting from its forehead. *A unicorn?* But those didn't exist. Kind of like vampires and werewolves.

Female laughter wisped around them. "Thaddeus, I knew you'd come to see me, the spirits told me, but they neglected to mention you'd bring such interesting friends."

"Hello, Circe. I see you still enjoy discomfiting newcomers."

Again, mirth swirled around them as the speaker remained hidden from sight. "A witch does what she can to amuse herself."

Witch? As in cauldron-stirring, cackling, magic-wielding, evil sorceress? Just when Toni thought she'd seen it all, more appeared. *Just how many secrets does our world hide under our very noses?*

Thaddeus rolled his eyes. "Could you amuse yourself another time? If the spirits have spoken, then you know we come on serious business."

"Ah yes, Morpheus and his plans to reform the world."

Did everyone know of this vampire and his mad plot?

With an almost audible *pop,* the setting before them vanished. Toni blinked. Gone was the disturbing home décor, replaced by a living room much like her grandmother used to own. Lamps with Tiffany shades illuminated the cozy space. Faded couches in burgundy velour draped with knitted afghans flanked a worn coffee table strewn with magazines—but not magazines found in the supermarket, unless they now carried *Chatewitch* or *Home and Cavern*. A fire snapped in a hearth, the wooden mantel above teeming with figurines, normal ones of cats cavorting, napping and posing.

In a rocking chair by the flames sat a young woman, or at least she appeared young. It took only one glance into her milky-white eyes for Toni to shiver and realize that, like Thaddeus, this woman was not human, and she was old. Really old, she'd wager.

"Won't you have a seat?" she offered with a wave of her hand.

"Thank you." Thaddeus seated himself on the longest of the couches, and in a domino effect, Toni sank down beside him, glued to his side, and Marc right next to her.

"Tea? Refreshments?"

It was Toni's intention to refuse, but Marc jumped in before she could. "Juice please, if you don't mind. And if you've got anything to eat, it would be welcome. Thad here tends to forget that some of us need food to survive."

"There were plenty of rabbits out in the garden if you were that famished, dog."

Circe clapped her hands. "Oh, how delightful. A male rivalry, and over a woman. How archaic and quaint. I've missed the duels gentlemen fought, and wars that men used to wage over the love of a female."

Toni blurted out, "Love? No love here. And they're not fighting because of me. They just don't like each other."

"Of course they're not, dear Antonia. Or may I call you Toni? I do so enjoy this century, with its cute habits of shortening perfectly respectable female names into masculine ones. So adorable."

So crazy. Toni wondered exactly why Thaddeus had brought them here. How could this crazy lady, sorry, witch, help them?

As if she read her mind, Circe smiled and said, "All will come clear. But first, have a snack. You must have strength for the battles ahead."

"Battles?" Thaddeus queried.

Good thing he could still speak because Toni couldn't. Her whole body froze in fascination as a platter floated into the room, stacked with sandwiches, crudités, cheese, and fruit. A jug of orange juice danced behind it with a pair of glasses trailing like little ducklings after their mother.

An empty glass bobbed in front of her.

"Come on now, grab it. It won't bite you, or at least this set of dishes won't. I keep those ones locked away for the guests I don't like." Circe's cupid-bow lips curved.

Not exactly reassuring, but given she didn't want to offend the crazy and powerful witch, Toni wrapped her fingers around the glass and managed not to squeak when the jug poured juice into it. After that, it was easy for her to accept the small plate piled with food, which settled on her lap.

The formalities taken care of, Circe nodded and said, "Excellent. I wouldn't want it bandied around that I was a poor hostess. Why, I'd have to leave my home and kill the speakers of such a vile rumor, and we all know how I hate to do that."

Toni made sure to eat an entire sandwich and make some appreciative noises.

Thaddeus tossed her an amused smile. She just glared as she chewed—on her second sandwich. A witch might have made them, but they were really tasty. Thick-cut honey ham layered with sharp cheddar and mustard on a fresh bun. She'd not realized her level of hunger until she fed it.

Marc was on his third sandwich before Circe seemed satisfied and deigned to answer Thaddeus.

"A war is coming, Thaddeus. One that threatens our existence."

"You are speaking of Morpheus and his plan to engage the Lycans by targeting the rogues."

"That is but the beginning. Morpheus is but a pawn in a bigger game, I fear."

"A game commanded by who?" Thaddeus asked.

"That I don't know. Whoever the mystery player is, he or she is cloaked."

"Hidden? From you?"

Toni paused in her nibbling of cheese at his surprise. She got the impression this was bad news.

"Yes, hidden from me." Circe couldn't hide her disgruntlement. "I've spent hours scrying. I've sent spirits spying. Yet, I can discover nothing."

"But you are sure they are behind Morpheus's

plan to start a war with the Lycans?"

"Morpheus or not, I think the Lycans would have come after the vampires anyway. What was done to Roderick, and what he, in turn, did to the wolves, has broken the fragile bond of peace between your kinds."

"But Nathan assured me he wanted nothing more than for his pack to exist in peace and recover from this."

"So he thinks. Now. But his mind will soon change. Many of them will as they face the reality of what Roderick did. The pack will demand justice for its lost loved ones. They will clamor for revenge, and the alpha will have no choice but to reply."

A disgusted noise blew past Thaddeus's lips. "Has everyone grown stupid? Have they all forgotten about the humans? The very technologically advanced humans, who are sure to notice if vampires and Lycans begin fighting?"

"Don't delude yourself. Discovery is only a *YouTube* cell phone video away. Change is coming, Thaddeus. It is up to you to decide what side you shall choose. Vampire. Wolf. Or…"

"Or what? Is there a third choice? A way to stop this?"

A rumble shook the house.

Toni grabbed for the plate on her lap before it fell, not that much remained on it. While Circe and Thaddeus spoke, she'd polished off its contents.

"What the hell was that?" Marc exclaimed. His eyes flashed yellow as the wolf rose to the surface, and Toni struggled against her own inner beast as it fought to break free, the overwhelming sense of danger sending it into a frenzy. *Let me out!*

"How dare they," Circe muttered as the house shuddered again. From elsewhere came the sound of breaking glass.

"Who is it? Who dares attack you?" Thaddeus asked. "Or should I say what?"

"You need to leave." Circe stood. Her youthful features hardened into an angry mask that added years to her appearance. She shooed them toward the front door. More breaking glass preceded the next round of tremors.

"What's going on?" Marc asked.

"It seems someone wants to pay me a visit, but not as a guest. We'll see about that," Circe grumbled.

"I will stay and aid you," Thaddeus offered.

"You will go and not look back. You will only get in my way. I am more than capable of handling the ghouls knocking at my foundation."

"Ghouls?" Toni squeaked. "How did they find us here?"

"The how does not matter. Just leave, so I might erect the house defenses."

Despite the fact that her feet didn't move, Toni and the guys found themselves standing by the front door. Circe had followed them, her milky-white orbs glowing with a blue radiance that highlighted her statically charged, floating hair.

"Thank you for the refreshments," Marc said as he yanked on the knob.

A tiny smile crossed Circe's lips. "Thank you for your courtesy, sir wolf. It's nice to finally meet a Lycan with manners. You may call on me again."

Not with me, he isn't. Toni didn't care for all the freakishness surrounding Circe.

The house rocked on its foundations again, and Circe scowled. "Daring scoundrels. I shall teach them."

Again, without volition, Toni and the boys moved in the blink of an eye, this time to find themselves alongside the car.

"Get in," Thad said brusquely, not at all perturbed by this odd method of locomotion.

"Shouldn't we help her?" Marc asked, gazing back at the house.

Circe stood framed in the doorway, light spilling out around her, hands raised and looking just like a witch should—freaky and all-powerful.

Both of Thaddeus's brows rose in astonishment, and he laughed. "And insult her?"

Movement from above drew Toni's attention, and she sucked in a breath as she caught sight of figures scuttling on the roof. "Ghouls," she whispered.

She wasn't the only one to have spotted them.

"Never fear. Circe can handle them," Thaddeus assured. "But there're too many for us. Now, get in before they change their focus and decide we are more worthwhile prey."

Marc practically shoved her into the vehicle.

Toni slid and scooted across the seat to leave

room for Marc, who dove in after her. The car door thudded shut. Thaddeus, already behind the wheel, started the engine and threw the car into reverse. He hit the gas and jolted them as he sped backward then, with an even bigger lurch that bounced her skull off the headrest, spun them around before slamming the car into forward gear. With a wild spin of the tires on loose gravel, he shot down the driveway, which she'd not noticed during their arrival because of her nap was bordered by thick and towering trees. A perfect cover for an—

"Ambush!" Marc yelled only a moment before the first body launched itself from a branch and hit the roof of their car. Thaddeus didn't slow down. On the contrary, she could hear the whine of the engine as he gave the vehicle more gas, hurtling them along the treacherous drive.

Another *thump* and a body landed on the hood. Toni watched in horrified fascination as the ghoul anchored himself by digging his claws in the body of the car before raising its head to glare at them. Red eyes and a slavering smile set her pulse pounding so ridiculously fast she feared she might suffer her first heart attack. Or wet her pants, given that the guy on the hood was the least of her problems. It seemed the ghoul on the roof wanted to come in, and he was pounding the hell out of the top of the car, dents appearing just above her head.

Toni didn't need anyone to tell her to duck. She unbuckled and slid between the seats, crouching close to the floor.

Marc also unbuckled but remained seated. "What are we going to do?"

"We can't stop and fight. We'll be outnumbered," Thaddeus replied. "If I can make it down this interminable driveway to the main road, we can hopefully make it to a clear spot and rid ourselves of the unwanted passengers."

"That's a lot of ifs," Marc pointed out.

"Do you have a better plan, dog?"

"Nah. But I thought I'd point out the flaws in yours, you know, in case I get a chance to say I told you so later."

"Noted. Now hold on. I'm going to try and make things a touch unpleasant for our guests and ensure we don't acquire new ones."

Somewhat forewarned, Toni braced herself and thus didn't get banged around too hard as Thaddeus swung the car to and fro, weaving them in a sickening, lurching pattern that resulted in the sound of screaming metal as the ghoul on the hood slipped a bit, his claws scraping on the hood. But he held on despite it all, even if he'd lost his grin.

As for the one above…

"Stay low," Marc yelled, just as a fist finally punched through the top of the car. The ghoul's victory was short-lived as Marc quickly grabbed ahold of the appendage and, with a sharp twist, cracked it.

Toni winced—that had to have hurt—and yet the monster seemed unaffected. Despite its hand flopping around on an obviously broken wrist, the arm thrust deeper into the vehicle as if desperate to grab ahold of them.

"The fucker is still going," Marc observed.

"Bite it off," Thaddeus advised, once again engaged in his swerving tactic.

Bite? She swallowed hard.

"I need room to shift. Toni, can you get in the front?"

The front? Which meant closer to the ghoul on the hood. Then again, judging by the arm dangling in the back, her current location wasn't any better.

"Don't let that thing touch me," she pleaded. Marc batted the dangling hand aside as she scrambled between the seats and flopped face-first onto the passenger seat. As she struggled to right herself, she heard more than saw Marc shift. Cloth tore, a sharp, musky scent enveloped the car, and Marc's painful grunt turned into a howl. Flipping her messy hair out of her eyes as she finally made it upright, Toni peeked over her shoulder to see a mass of auburn fur filled the backseat.

"Close your eyes," Thaddeus advised.

Not questioning, she shut them tight but couldn't stem the meaty sound of teeth tearing into flesh and bone. A foul stink filled the car, a stink she recognized from the hotel as ghoul. Circe's lovely sandwiches roiled in her tummy.

Thump. Thump.

"Excellent. We've lost one," Thaddeus announced.

A sharp bark from behind her seemed to echo

his observation. In her head, her own wolf seemed indignant they'd not had a chance to help.

Sit down and behave. Just because her wolf thought it would be fun to fight some ghouls didn't mean Toni was on board.

Although she might not have a choice. The monster on the hood seemed determined to stick around. Inch by inch, he clawed his way closer to the windshield, digging his talons into the metal, dragging himself forward, a mountain climber determined to make it to his destination.

But while the ghoul strove to his goal, they'd made theirs. Thaddeus hit the main road and, with a squeal of tires and a spin of the wheels, fishtailed them onto it.

The monster's body swayed, but its claws kept it anchored.

"Hold on, little wolf. Time to put some distance between us and this guy's friends."

It was a good thing the backwoods road they found themselves on didn't have any cops at this hour because Thaddeus went well beyond the speed limit. Heck, he almost pushed them past the car's limit, given how the engine screamed as the RPMs went well into the red.

"Brace yourself" was the only warning she got before they went from Mach speed to stopped. Toni, who'd buckled in, still felt her body heave forward and her neck snap.

Before she could decide if she hurt or not, she heard car doors opening and a vicious snarl. Raising her head, she could only stare as Thaddeus strode without hesitation to a heap on the ground several yards in front of them. In the glare of the headlights, she saw the ghoul, thrown from the hood, make it to its feet, only to go down as a blur of red fur tackled it.

She shut her eyes after that, even though her wolf urged her to watch and learn. Some things she didn't need to visualize. Reaching out blindly, she cranked the music in the car, all the better to ignore what happened outside, not that the ghoul screamed.

When her door clicked open, she didn't immediately look up, proving once again the adage that when you assumed, *You make an ass with U and me.* The smell hit her before the hand that grabbed her by the hair, but by the time she reacted and screamed, the ghoul had already dragged her out of the car.

And her wolf went ballistic!

Chapter Twenty-Four

Thaddeus sensed the danger a moment too late. He whirled from what remained of the ghoul's body, more slabs of meat to be tossed in the woods for scavengers than man, but even he wasn't fast enough to stop the attack.

Somehow they'd missed a passenger. Another ghoul, wearing signs of road rash, swayed by the passenger door of his car. Toni, eyes shut, was completely oblivious to its presence.

Thaddeus began to run, Marc a furry companion at his side, but they both knew they wouldn't make it in time.

The creature opened the door, and Thaddeus, panicked for the first time in decades, didn't think to send a mental warning to Toni, but shouted one, "Look out."

Not that she heard him over her scream of pain and surprise. It didn't matter. The ghoul might have begun by yanking out a human woman riveted by fear, but he ended up facing a snarling, very unhappy wolf. Thaddeus slowed his steps as Toni or, more accurately, her beast, unleashed some pent-up anger on the creature.

Instinct drove her to attack the thing's throat, her weight and savagery, driving it to the ground. She ravaged it and ignored the hands that sought to beat her back. While Thaddeus was content to let her fight her own battle until she showed signs of needing help, Marc seemed determined to aid her.

Still wearing his wolf skin, Marc dove at the ghoul's arm, a powerful bite and several shakes of his head tearing it loose. The ghoul didn't stand a chance. It was only a matter of moments before the Lycans rendered it into pieces perfect for disposal. And enough to horrify the woman hidden within the wolf.

Linked in a way he didn't fully understand, Thaddeus could feel both the wolf's exultation at conquering the enemy and Toni's disgust at what she'd just done. With time wasting, he could only send her a mental reassurance—*all is well, you did what you had to*—before more pressing matters claimed him, such as disposing of the evidence.

While Thaddeus grabbed the still twitching limbs and flung them into the forest for the scavengers, Marc lugged his own chunks to the nearby ditches and used his hind legs to pile dirt and debris partially over them, hiding them from casual view.

By the time anyone happened across them, Thaddeus and his band of merry wolves—if one could call a pair a band—would be long gone.

Bodies disposed of, there was just one dilemma, make that two. One, his car wasn't in any shape to go anywhere too public. With a ravaged hood and roof, it would draw too much attention. But his other dilemma was how to fit two wolves in his car? For some reason, the idea of having the pair of them seated in the vehicle, heads hanging out the window, tongues lolling, had him almost laughing. Almost. He didn't entirely lose track of the direness of their situation.

Someone had balls big and brazen enough to attack them in what should have been a safe place. Circe portended war and change. Dawn fast approached. And he'd ruined yet another pair of Armani slacks and Gucci loafers. Not to mention, his wolf companions had torn through their clothes. Good thing he had spares in his trunk.

One problem solved, at least. As for the rest? He needed a place to hunker for the day, a place they could drive to quickly and without drawing attention. He and his companions needed to regroup, make plans, and shower. Ghoul guts did not make for a pleasant odor.

But first…Thaddeus approached Toni who paced back and forth at the edge of the road, eyeing the forest but luckily not bounding off into its shadows. Good thing. He didn't have time to chase her down. At least it displayed Toni gaining some measure of control over her beast.

Marc attempted to approach her, and she bared her teeth. She did the same to Thaddeus, who ignored the attempted brush-off. He knelt in front of the large dark creature and made sure he caught her gaze.

"Hello, little wolf. Or should I say big wolf? Quite the big beautiful creature you were hiding inside."

She tossed her head, her savage side recognizing the compliment.

"Good job protecting yourself," he continued as if he spoke to animals every day. He used his most soothing tone, calming the adrenaline he sensed still coursing through her system.

"What are you doing?" Marc asked, having shifted while he talked Toni down.

"Having a conversation with Antonia. I was just about to tell her how brave it was of her to take on that ghoul. You kicked its evil carcass."

"Damned straight she did. I knew she could." Marc's tone projected pride, and Toni's wolf relaxed even further, the bristling fur settling.

"Doesn't it feel good to know you're not defenseless? Not anymore. I know you were scared, anyone would be faced with a danger, especially a surprise attack like that, but you handled it like a pro."

As he watched, the body before him rippled, contorted, limbs cracked as hair receded until a naked and panting Toni knelt before him. "Pro?" she gasped. "You call chewing out a monster's throat and severing limbs professional?"

Thaddeus shrugged. "It got the job done."

"And I need a toothbrush," she complained, leaning to the side and spitting in a very unladylike fashion.

"Would a mint do for the moment?" Thaddeus asked, tendering her a Tic-Tac.

She took the plastic box and rattled it before

arching an amused brow. "You carry around breath mints?"

"Of course. Any self-respecting vampire does. You know blood breath is as bad as garlic."

She snorted. Then laughed, collapsing on the ground on her bare bottom and giving in to hysterical mirth while Marc eyed her with his head on a tilt.

"I'll never understand women," Marc muttered.

"I've lived centuries and still don't, but their very mystery is what makes them special." Thaddeus offered Toni a hand, and she took it, letting him pull her to her feet.

To his surprise, she didn't move away, but closer, wrapping her arms around his torso and resting her head on his chest.

"I was so scared," she admitted.

Returning her hug, Thaddeus reassured her. "Yet you didn't let fear rule you. You fought back."

"As a wolf."

"You used the weapon you had to best effect."

"I've never hurt someone before, never imagined I'd be able to."

"In a perfect world, you wouldn't have to. Alas, perfection must always be balanced by darkness that we might better appreciate it when we do come across it."

"Aren't you just the poet?" she sniffled against his shirt.

Over her shoulder, Marc rolled his eyes. Thaddeus tossed him a cold smirk and mouthed,

Jealous? The glower was answer enough.

"We probably shouldn't stand here in the road, especially given we're covered in blood and two of us are naked," Marc stated.

Toni's face buried deeper as she groaned. "Dammit. I burst out of my clothes."

"We have spares."

In short order, everyone was dressed and they were en route with a mashed-up car. In a stroke of luck, Sasha hooked him up with a residence in the area—after she finished laughing about his predicament.

Before the dawn's rays could kiss the sky, they were pulling into a secluded driveway for a lakeside getaway, a cottage residence if one could consider a sprawling, five-thousand-foot home with six bedrooms a retreat.

The lockbox on the side door opened without a hitch, and they entered the home, belonging to a friend of Sasha's—a wealthy one judging by the decor—and hopefully safe for the moment.

"I'm starved," Marc announced as he headed for the kitchen.

"Me too," Toni stated in surprise. "Is that normal?"

"Shifting takes a lot of energy," Marc explained as he rummaged through the cupboards in search of sustenance.

The third one yielded canned goods, including some hearty soup, which was soon warming in the microwave.

Bedraggled, but alive and uninjured. Thaddeus mused aloud, "It seems this quest has taken a dangerous turn. If you and the wolf still wish to run and hide, I won't stop you."

"But…" Toni hesitated, gnawing at her lower lip as if in thought. "I thought your plan was to keep me."

"It was."

"So why the change of heart?"

"Before, I feared you were susceptible to mind control. I didn't want to see you become a victim again. That's no longer a concern, and tonight you proved yourself capable of defending yourself."

"So now that I'm not some fragile damsel in need of protection, you don't want me?"

"Of course not. I want you. Never doubt that, little wolf. I want you right now, on this table. On this counter. Hell, I'd even take you with the wolf, if that's what would make you happy."

"Then why are you telling me to leave?"

"To keep you safe. As you saw and heard tonight, there are grave matters afoot. War and change are coming. I can't guarantee your safety with me, not given I'm a target."

Her lips tightened into a stubborn line he was coming to recognize. "And if I won't go?"

She'd stay? With him? To his shock, a warm emotion he'd not felt in decades, perhaps even centuries, swelled his heart.

"What do you mean you won't go?" Marc asked from where he leaned on the counter, a silent watcher until now.

"Like it or not, I'm now a part of this. Wasn't it you who said I couldn't hide from who I was? What I am? Well, I'm wolf, Lycan, whatever you want to call it. With a dash of fucked-up vampire. I'm also a chickenshit who still managed to kick some ghoul ass, and my momma raised me right. I'm not going to run off like a coward and let Thaddeus try to save the world on his own."

"You're going to stay?"

She nodded, and Thaddeus found himself bereft of words for once. How long since someone had done something to aid him with no expectation?

"And what about me?"

Toni held out her hand to him. "I hope you'll stay with me. With us."

"What are you saying?" Marc seemed determined to have her verbalize it, but Thaddeus, still in tune to a certain extent with her mind and emotions, could read her.

She wants both of us. The catch was the words were caught in her throat. "I—Uh—" Toni peered at him for help.

Thaddeus, who couldn't help himself where she was concerned, ignored his urge to kill the competition and gave her what she wanted. "What she's trying to say, mutt, is she desires us both. She wants us both. You. Me. Her. Not exactly the trio your pack laws planned for, but what her heart, and her body, wants."

It took Mark a moment to digest this, a long

moment before he asked. "Is this true?"

She nodded.

He sighed. "This is majorly fucked up."

"Eloquently put," Thaddeus mocked wryly.

"I'm sorry. I can't help how I feel." She blushed and stared at her feet.

Before the moment could become too awkward, Thaddeus decided to save it. "Sasha told me the basement, which is vampire friendly, apparently has a large shower, a very large shower. I don't know about you, but I could use one before sleep. Shall we?" Thaddeus held a hand out to her, and Toni, despite the arousal coursing through her veins, hesitated.

Would she change her mind?

Chapter Twenty-Five

The moment had arrived. A moment she'd vaguely fantasized about, especially since Marc planted in her head the idea of being with two men. Thing was he'd meant wolves, and despite his fangs, Thaddeus was definitely no canine.

However, he was right when he said she wanted him. Wanted him and his darkness. Him and his take-charge, no-bullshit attitude. Just like she wanted Marc, so desperate to keep her safe. Mark who'd shown himself gentle and caring and so obviously willing to do anything for her.

Polar opposites, in looks and temperament, yet they both called to something in her. She wasn't sure yet if she wanted a forever after with them. She did know that her body desperately craved release. She needed a physical connection, and an emotional one, to these two men.

Was it the fact that they'd fought a few times and faced death that made her feel this way? Was it her new Lycan side changing who she was, making her want more out of life than just a mundane nine-to-five existence? Or was it something more? Something…fated. Special. *Love?*

The reason didn't really matter. The moment was here. Now. Her opportunity to take a step into a new world, new experience. No one knew what tomorrow would bring. Would she even survive to see next month? If she didn't take this step in a brave new direction, would she forever lose the moment? Would she regret not attempting what promised to be the erotic adventure of a lifetime?

She slid her hand into Thad's and held out her free hand to Marc.

His eyes caught hers, and he mouthed, "Are you sure?"

She nodded. A grin tugged the corner of her mouth. "Yeah, but no biting. Yet. And let's go easy on the really wild stuff. I might not be a virgin, but two guys and me? Not exactly my usual bedroom dynamic."

"Then you're in for a sensual treat," Thad declared. He pulled out his cell phone and read something before he punched in a code on a keypad by a door in the kitchen. It clicked before it swung open. "Shall we? According to Sasha's message, we're safest downstairs."

Time to enter the lair. Toni bit back a giggle as she followed Thad through the entrance to the basement.

The door sealed shut behind them with an ominous *click,* and each step down the softly lit staircase into the bowels of the house echoed in rhythm with the too-loud thump of her heart.

The steps spilled out into a large living space, recessed lighting in the ceiling giving it a warm glow while the scattered furniture made it seem both cozy and comfortable. A flick of a switch and a fireplace ignited.

"Is this house owned by a vampire?" she asked, not really caring but needing to do something in the silence lest her nerves have her dancing a jig.

"Not quite. But according to Sasha, the host often has guests who are keen on security, privacy, and darkness, hence the accommodations."

"So where's the bathroom and the shower? I can't wait to sluice off," Marc remarked.

Sluice or…

She cast him a glance, and her cheeks heated at the smoldering look he aimed her way. Peeking at Thaddeus did nothing to alleviate it because he bore an equally sensual, yet hungry, gaze.

The first door led to a small kitchen area replete with fridge and microwave. The second, a large bedroom done in dark blue with silver accents. The lush shag carpet begged for bare toes, and Toni gladly shed her shoes to sink them in.

"Gosh, that's soft," she murmured.

"Not as soft as your skin, I'll wager" was Thad's reply. He followed up his compliment with a soft kiss dropped on her lips. She caught her breath. He tugged her to an open arch, where the gleam of white subway and glass tile beckoned.

"Wow." Marc's exclaimed word aptly described the bathroom, a large space dominated by a huge glass-enclosed shower.

She counted. "Twelve showerheads? Who needs that many?"

Thad chuckled. "That's nothing. At the

compound, the master bedroom facilities boast sixteen, plus a rain shower one overhead."

Before she could ask how dirty he got, hands tugged at her clothes. Thaddeus wasted no time. Shyness returned as she wondered what the heck she was doing. Was this the right thing to do? Was she—

Lips claimed hers, Marc's this time, their softness easing her tenseness, his touch stoking the fire within. While Marc thoroughly explored her mouth, Thaddeus stripped her, his lean fingers stroking lightly across the skin he bared, leaving frissons of desire wherever he touched.

It took but moments to bare her and only seconds more until her bareness was covered by the nakedness of her partners.

One for the front. One for the back. Under their guidance, she made it to the shower, the soft patter of warm water not diminishing her ardor in the least. On the contrary, they made bathing into a sensory delight as four soapy hands took to lathering and exploring every inch of her. When she would have swooned, her legs wobbly and unwilling to hold her up, Marc became the solid presence at her back, leaning her into his chest, his arms looped around her and holding her upright.

On his knees before her, an oddly supplicant position she would have never imagined for Thaddeus, he meticulously bathed her lower stomach, dragging a sudsy cloth over its round form, over her wide hips. He circled the cloth around and down her thighs, left then right, avoiding in his ministrations the one area screaming for his touch. When he got to her toes and tickled them in his quest to bathe her, she did protest.

"You're killing me here," she moaned.

Marc, busy nibbling on her ear, chuckled, the sound vibrating her sensitive lobe. "Hey, Thad, isn't there a French expression for pleasure that involves dying?"

Dark eyes, with a tiny pinprick of red, a color she'd come to appreciate as she now associated it with excitement and not pain, at least when Thad wore it, met hers. "Ah yes, *la petite mort*, an eloquent way of saying climax. Something you'll be enjoying several of."

"Soon, I hope," she grumbled as the idle chitchat meant no one was kissing or stroking.

A crooked smile made Thad appear almost boyish. "Patience, little wolf. I've imagined this moment since we met. I intend to savor it."

"Don't worry. I'm getting as impatient as you," Marc growled in her ear. He cupped her face and turned it for a scorching kiss, his tongue melding with hers.

Toni kissed him back with hunger, sucking on his tongue, fighting an urge to bite. Erotic release wasn't the only thing riding her at the moment. A savage need to mark kept distracting her, but Toni was the boss of her body. Kind of.

When Thaddeus nipped the flesh just below her belly button, her hips arched, and molten heat made her pussy pulse. But he was just beginning. He rubbed his cheek and jaw against her flesh, dragging the rough bristles of his midnight shadow on her skin. Lower. Lower still.

Distracted, she forgot to kiss Marc, but he didn't seem to mind, as he busied himself kneading her full breasts while kissing her neck. She trembled from head to toe as Thad's mouth finally reached the spot begging for attention and hovered. He blew on her softly, and she couldn't help but cry out and arch again, wantonly begging for him to lick.

A quiver went through her sex, and moisture pooled. His hands spread her thighs, and she clenched in anticipation, but he tortured her, embracing the tender skin of her inner thigh, rubbing his rough jaw around the edges of her nether lips. He blew on her sensitized nub, a nub that throbbed, ripe and ready for his tongue.

"Please." She couldn't help but whimper; her need was so strong.

"Sweet, little wolf, so eager. So beautiful." He paused and gave her a long, wet lick, anticipated so long it almost made her come. "So, *tasty*," he purred before he finally placed his mouth on her sex.

About time. And oh, was it worth it. His hot tongue bathed her pussy, following the outline of her lips, jabbing at the opening, then flicking at her clit. Toni's hips thrashed but not for long, as Marc's hands anchored her and kept her upright and spread, a feast for Thad to enjoy.

Through heavily lidded eyes, she stared down at

Thad's dark crown. As if sensing her stare, he paused in his oral enjoyment. His eyes, lit with passion, peered up at her. His lips curved into a sensual smile.

"I think it's time the wolf got a turn."

Thaddeus stood, his erection, long, lean and straining, jutting from his body. Caught staring at it, she didn't immediately protest when Thad grabbed her hands and secured them over her head, pushing her back against the warm tile of the shower.

Marc wasted no time. He dropped to his knees, and his mouth locked onto her pussy while Thaddeus bent his head to capture the tip of a nipple.

Arousal raced through her. Restrained, and pleasured by two mouths at once, she couldn't escape their touch, not that she wanted to. The pleasure was incredible. Insane. Too much.

With a scream to almost shatter glass, she came, the force of her orgasm so intense that, yes, like the French claimed, she probably died for a moment.

But what a way to go.

Her climax didn't signal the end of the fun. On the contrary, it brought things to the next level, a level that involved her being enveloped in a huge fluffy towel and carried to the massive bed in the next room.

The minor cooldown didn't discourage them in the least. In short order, the towel was whisked away, but she didn't feel the cold. On the contrary, heat made her writhe as they took turns with her, one sucking on her nipples, pulling and tugging them into aching peaks. The other feasted on her body's honey, nestled between her legs, tongue lapping and bringing her back to the brink.

She'd given up trying to keep track of who did what and let herself just bask in the sensation. Four hands, two mouths, coinciding desires, all in one place, all intent on one goal; her pleasure.

How selfish, and yet when she tried to grasp them, fingers managing a fleeting caress, a tug, the erection was whisked out of reach with a chiding, "Not yet. We're not done with you."

Who knew Thaddeus hid such a sensual tease underneath his dark persona?

Her second climax approached. Her breathing was an erratic mess, her shower ruined by the perspiring flush covering her from head to toe. She arched on the brink of satisfaction, and that was when they finally decided to take a turn.

With a final lick, the mouth latched onto her nipple released it with a soft, wet *pop*. She opened heavy lids to see Thaddeus kneeling beside her head on the bed. His hand stroked his erect penis, the length of it almost daunting, almost. She'd always wondered if longer truly was better. She couldn't wait to find out.

Mesmerized by the motion of his hand sliding up and down his shaft—squeezing, releasing, the cadence almost hypnotic—she didn't realize Marc had poised himself between her thighs. But she soon felt it. The tip of his cock pushed against her nether lips. If she thought Thad was long, Marc was wide. Very wide. She cast a glance at him to peek and sucked in a breath. *Will he fit?*

He answered the question in a fell swoop as he sheathed himself.

"Oh, dear God," she moaned as he stretched her. It was tight. So damned tight. But good, oh so good. Her eyes almost rolled back in her head at the sensation of fullness.

And she wasn't the only one to appreciate it.

"You are so fucking tight and perfect, Toni," grunted Marc as he stroked in and out of her. His thickly muscled body glistened with perspiration. But apparently he wasn't getting the angle he wanted because his hands pushed at her legs, hoisting them until they rested on his shoulders, seating him even deeper inside.

He'd found her sweet spot. Toni gasped and clawed at the sheets as the head of his fat cock bumped against her G-spot. Over and over, he ground against it while Toni thrashed and tried to meet his strokes, out of her mind with the rapture he wrung from her body.

The urge to mark this man, to draw him to her and bite the corded column of his neck rode her hard. She could even imagine the salty taste. She growled and reached for him, but he chose that moment to arch back with a groaned, "Here it comes." Marc thrust one final time and held himself rigid as his cock spurted hotly.

Toni couldn't help but mewl in complaint when

he withdrew because, while he'd found his pleasure, she was still on the peak of hers. Good thing she had a second lover ready to take over.

Where Marc's cock was wide, Thad's was long and fully erect, curved at the end. Slim, but strong fingers gripped her thighs, holding her wide open so he could pin her with his penis. She arched off the bed. If she'd thought Marc hit the spot, his was only a tease compared to what Thad could do. Piston-like in motion, Thad pumped into her, his cock striking her G-spot with unerring precision with each stroke. Already at the edge, Toni climaxed, her body shaking and shuddering with the strength of her release. Her hoarse cries were caught by Marc as he kissed her.

Thad came, but she didn't actually perceive it. It was more like she heard it within her mind, a very masculine and pleased, *Mine!* A feeling she understood all too well. It seemed it wasn't just Marc she wanted to bite but Thad too. And stranger, the idea of them biting her back, marking and claiming her as their woman, appealed as well.

If she could have spoken more than gibberish, she might have asked them to. As it was, sated and feeling sexier than at any other point in her life, she knew there'd be a next time, a time to say, "Yes, mark me." In that moment, she didn't doubt they cared for her, didn't worry about her wide hips or the fact she'd just made love to two men. She did what any woman would do after mind-blowing sex with two men. She snuggled between them, one at her back spooning, one at her front, forehead touching hers.

Sandwiched, warm and safe, she went to sleep with a smile on her lips.

Chapter Twenty-Six

This time Toni recognized the setting for what it was: a dream. *I just wish I could choose a nicer location, say like a five-star resort.* But no, her subconscious apparently harbored a sadistic side, and once again, she found herself in her dreary cell, wearing a gauzy nightgown trimmed with red hearts and ribbons. Ready for a lover…or two.

Unlike her last visit, this time the door to her prison was open. A shame, she'd quite enjoyed Thaddeus's appearance, and Marc's. They'd opened her eyes in this dreamscape to the possibilities, and now that they'd shown them to her, she had to wonder why she'd held back.

But back to her dream. Why was she here? Was there something to be learned? Done? Only one way to find out.

She strode from her former cell, the silence around her oppressive but not threatening. It seemed the fear she'd lived with for so long was losing its grip. Apparently eating some dead guy's ashes, kicking some ghoul butt, and then having the courage to take two men in hand—and in her body—did a lot for a girl's self-esteem.

If I can handle that, I can handle anything. Cocky, perhaps, but it beat the alternative of jumping at her own shadow. She no longer feared the vampires.

Her mind was her own. She had the strength to fight back and the strength to make a choice. Getting involved with two guys was because she wanted it, on her terms, and not because she needed to hide behind them for their protection.

And was she ever glad she'd chosen them both.

It seemed prudish in retrospect for her to have dismissed the idea of having two men in her bed and heart. *Two certainly made it a lot more fun.*

Yet while it left her feeling content, what about the two guys? Thaddeus was old and probably set in his ways. Would he really want to involve himself with a wolf who came with a partner? And what about her Lycan partner? He might claim that Pack Law dictated the need for more than one in her life, but he'd probably never counted on it being not only a stranger but a vampire. *Yes, I quite enjoyed it. Yes, I'd like to do it again, but what about them?* How did they feel about it?

Judging by the glum countenance of the one who sat outside the prison house on the front step, she wasn't sure if Marc would want a repeat.

Toni seated herself beside Marc. "Dream hopping again?"

He tossed her a smile as he placed his arm around her for a hug. "So it seems. I hope you don't mind. For some reason I found myself here."

"I guess you could call this our spot. It is, after all, where we first met." She wrinkled her nose. "Although we really should do something about sprucing the place up. Maybe get a few garden gnomes. A pink flamingo."

He chuckled. "Can you imagine Thad's face if you did that to his garden? I'll bet he's the type of guy to have straight rows and perfectly spaced flowers."

"And no weeds," she added.

"Definitely no weeds. Damn, now I want to hit a Walmart and find the tackiest lawn ornament ever and see what he does."

She joined him laughing. "He'd probably have a little fit."

"A little?" Marc angled a brow.

"Okay, a lot."

"But he'd let you keep it," Marc admitted. "For a vampire, he seems awfully smitten with you."

"And me with him. I'm also quite smitten with you." Somehow admitting her feelings in the dreamscape was so much easier than in person. The ethereal feel took some of the anxiety from it and made it easier to speak honestly.

"I like you a lot too, Toni." Marc also seemed to have found his tongue. "Which is why I've got to ask you to leave."

"Leave?" She drew away from him.

"Yes, leave. You heard that weird witch and Thad. Things are going to hell. Just the three of us can't hope to prevail. You're not safe."

"It's not just us three. Thad has Sasha and some others."

"But not enough to stop the coming violence."

She pointed out the flaw in his logic. "So you

think you're too few, yet you think I'd be safer alone?"

"No, which is why I think we need to talk again about you joining a pack."

"Assuming any would take me, not that it matters. I'm not leaving."

Marc uttered a noise of frustration and in his agitation ran a hand through his hair. "You are stubborn."

"Loyal."

"But I'm scared for you," he whispered.

"I'm scared for us all, but I'd rather we face this together." She placed her hand on his thigh, and he covered it with his hand.

"We need allies," Marc grumbled.

"I agree," said her vampire lover.

Toni didn't even flinch when Thaddeus joined the conversation. She'd expected he'd eventually show up. "Took you long enough," she sassed.

"A little she-wolf wrung me out. I needed to recover before I had the strength to join the party." Thaddeus shot her a slow, sensual smile, but after all they'd done, it would take more than that to make her blush.

"So what should we do to start amassing an army of our own?" Marc asked.

"I believe, with the information we now have, it's time to contact Nathan again. As head of the Lycan council and one of the largest packs, he would prove invaluable to have on our side. I will do that when we waken."

"How about your friend Sasha? Any idea how's she doing?" Toni asked.

"I checked my phone before following you into dreamland and heard from her."

"Did she find any of Roderick's wolves?"

"Yes, none of the crazy ones though. Those seem to have vanished, which, needless to say, doesn't bode well. However, she did manage to corner a handful of sane ones in a town. They'd banded together, survivors sticking in a group and all that."

"They didn't harm her or the others?"

"No, but she says it took some fast talking before they'd listen."

"What's she doing with them?" Marc asked.

"Taking them to that compound I told you of, which is also where we'll head once the sun sets."

"We're leaving the area? We're not going back to find more of the rogues?"

Thaddeus shook his head. "I don't know how refined your mental tracking is, or if you even got any from Roderick's ashes, but I can tell you, for my part, that the tenebrous link I had to several of the roaming minions is no longer there. Whether dead, enthralled to another, or turned I can't tell, though."

"We're too late?"

"Too late for them. So there's no point in sticking around and fleeing from spot to spot."

"That sucks," Marc grumbled. "Ever feel like we're constantly one step behind?"

"Yes, which is why we're going to retreat."

"You mean run away and head to this house of yours. What are we going to do there?"

"It's time we prepared our defenses and dug in for the upcoming conflict. By choosing our ground for battle, we can better control events and the outcome."

"Or make ourselves into sitting targets," Marc added.

"I assure you the one thing we won't be is targets. The location is almost a bunker of sorts, with security cameras, motion sensors, automated shutters, which, when dropped over the openings of the house, are bullet and bombproof."

"Readying for an Armageddon, were you?" Marc asked.

"Call it self-preservation. I've got a few of these secure locations scattered around the world in case of emergencies."

"If you had somewhere to hunker down until the shit blew over, why get involved in the first place? If you had a place to run and hide, why not let the Lycans and the vampires duke it out?"

"For the same reason Toni won't let you tuck her away. Sometimes you have to take a stand and fight back."

Toni reached out a hand, and when Thaddeus slipped his into it, she tugged at him until he sat with her on the step. She laced her other hand with Marc's. "Sitting back and watching when we could possibly make a difference isn't an option. But I do know that together we stand a better chance of succeeding."

Marc chuckled. "I'll admit that theory worked in the bedroom and shower, but what makes you think it will transfer to a battle?"

She drew their clasped hands to her lips and kissed them both. "Because now we all have someone and something to fight for."

Chapter Twenty-Seven

Wakening to one side of Toni, while Thad slumbered on the other, didn't freak Marc out as much as he feared. What began as a dislike and rivalry with the vampire had transitioned. He wouldn't exactly claim to like the guy, but he did have more respect for him and could now see him as a person instead of just a vampire. It also helped that Toni made it clear she wanted both of them, or neither of them. She wouldn't tolerate jealous bickering. Or, as she told them when they entered into a staring, growling match, "Behave, or I'll take my pussy and play with it myself." Nothing like the threat of no sex to calm them the fuck down. Then again, Marc wasn't serious about staking the bloodsucker and sticking him out in the sun for a tan, but a guy had to have some fun.

Easing out of the bed, careful to let her eke out as many minutes of sleep as possible, Marc took first turn in the shower then headed off to scrounge up some breakfast. Within a half-hour, Toni arrived in the kitchen, her hair wet and skin still dewy. A wan-looking Thaddeus was last to appear, circles under his eyes and his skin paler than usual.

Marc frowned. Someone looked like he'd gotten hit with a hangover truck. "What's up with you?"

"A tad peckish. But I'll survive. I've got blood

stored at the compound to feed me once we arrive."

Toni bit her lip. "Are you sure you can wait that long?"

"I'll live, or not, depending on your view of my kind," was Thad's reply.

"I guess I could loan you some of mine." She held out her arm.

To Marc's surprise, Thaddeus shook his head. "I can sense your fear and hesitation at the thought, so while I appreciate the offer, no. I'll be fine. It won't be the first time I've gone hungry for a day or two, and I'm sure it won't be the last."

And once again, an opportunity for the vampire to prove himself a dick wasted as Thaddeus put Toni's needs above his own. *If I'm not careful, I might start respecting him.* Wouldn't that be fucked up?

As Marc and Toni polished off their breakfast—Chef Boyardee Ravioli in a can with spray cheese on top—Thaddeus dug out his phone and dialed a number.

"Morning, dog."

The sneer in Thaddeus's tone took Marc by surprise. When was the last time he'd heard it used against him? A while, apparently. A sign Thad was beginning to see him in a different light? Or just an indication of his dislike for Nathan, whom Marc had met only briefly but, from all accounts, was an alpha through and through, tough, a bit of an asshole, and not welcoming to outsiders, especially non-Lycan ones.

Despite the tinny sound on the cell phone, he

didn't have a problem hearing Nathan's reply.

"If it isn't the UV-challenged one. Darkness has fallen, and you can now come out and play?"

"You would do well to watch your mockery, wolf. I am in no mood for it, and when you hear my news, you'll see why."

"More dire predictions, I take it? Or just plain paranoia? We've had nothing happen over here. No missing persons. No psychotic episodes. Oh, and no army of darkness at our compound walls."

"Yet. I thought you might wish to know that the missing rogues have been claimed or killed by sources unknown."

"One thing less to worry about, I guess."

The nonchalance in Nathan's reply bothered Marc, and he got a sense this conversation was headed downhill fast.

Thad gritted his teeth. "Not exactly reason to celebrate. We have reason to believe that a vampire is turning the missing wolves into ghouls."

"And what exactly is a ghoul?"

"Think half zombie, half vampire, a whole lot of nuts, whose sole purpose is death and chaos."

Succinct, yet eloquent. Marc almost applauded. Toni paced in worry, and Marc motioned for her to move closer. She did, right onto his lap. He slipped his arm around her waist in reassurance.

A whistle came from the earpiece of the phone. "Holy fuck, sounds like your coven, or whatever you call yourselves, is having some serious issues."

"Issues that affect us all."

"Is this your way of saying you expect me and my pack to help you?"

Again, Thaddeus ground his teeth. "It would behoove you to, yes."

"Sounds to me like it's an internal problem. Vampire politics, power grabbing and whatnot. I don't see why we should get involved." Nathan's sneer came through loud and clear.

"Why? Because they are using wolves to create an army of ghouls."

"Outcasts, who by their deeds are not welcome. Rogues who lack the mentality to protect themselves. What do I care what happens to them?"

Marc frowned at this. Since when did the Pack turn on its own? Yes, the missing wolves were rogues, but not by choice. With Roderick gone, didn't they deserve a second chance? Perhaps Nathan wasn't comfortable dealing with a vampire. Marc gestured for the phone. With a shrug, Thaddeus handed it over.

"Nathan? Hi, it's Marc. I'm a—I mean I was a friend of Trent and Darren."

"You survived." Flatly said.

Marc ignored the foreboding forming a ball in his stomach. "Yeah, I got my mind back, and I'm real sorry for what happened. I've been doing my best to try and make up for it. I rescued one of Roderick's victims, a dormant female that he activated. She's actually with me right now."

"That's good news." Nathan's tone warmed slightly. "She's under your protection?"

"Yes, but I'd like to bring her by at one point to see how Pack life works. Being new and all, she's still coming to grips with the whole Lycan deal."

The warmth didn't last. The hard-assed alpha came back. "Sorry, Marc. Not happening. You and the female aren't welcome here, or in any other pack for that matter."

Icy fingers of dread stalked up his spine. "What do you mean not welcome? I assure you, we're completely sane."

"Says the guy working with a vampire," was Nathan's sarcastic reply.

"A vampire who saved our asses."

"Lucky you."

"I can assure you Thad's not a bad dude. Arrogant prick, yes, but he seems sincere about helping us against the rogues turned ghoul."

"I'm sure he is, but he's still a vampire. How do I know he hasn't fucked with your mind?"

"Because he hasn't." And couldn't.

"Let's say, for argument's sake, you're not compelled or harboring some sick vampire time bomb in your head. I still wouldn't let you in. None of the wolves Roderick touched are welcome."

"Since when? I know for a fact your pack took some of the wolves under Roderick's dominion into your care."

"Yes, we did and, for the most part, regretted it. Of the two dozen or so we captured, only a few retained their wits. The rest, well, let's just say, they're proving more trouble than they're worth. At least those not in a vegetative state."

"So what are you going to do? Kill them all?" A pregnant pause followed Marc's exaggeration. Or was it the truth? "Holy fuck. You're going to execute them."

"It's the only humane thing we can do," Nathan tried to explain. "It sounds like you survived your time at Roderick's hands. You, Jaxon, the girl you found, and a few others. But I'm telling you, the rest, they're…" Nathan trailed off as if searching for words. "They're evil. I know it sounds crazy, but there's something in their eyes that makes my danger radar tingle. I can't have them putting the Pack in jeopardy."

"So set them free."

"I can't. I don't trust them. And if what you and this Thaddeus dude says is true, I wouldn't be freeing them so much as making them easy prey for whomever is using them in their plot for power in the vampire world."

"But to kill them…It's genocide."

"It's necessary."

Anger made him brash. "So if I came back, does this mean you'd kill me too?"

"Put it this way. I wouldn't recommend showing up at our gates."

"You'd kill me!" Marc couldn't help his note of astonishment. Banished was one thing, but to place a death sentence on him? "But I'm not fucking crazy."

"Says the guy who's hooked up with a vampire.

Sorry, but I can't take a chance with my pack."

Marc already considered himself outcast. By choice. He'd made the decision after Roderick's death, but a part of him had hoped that perhaps one day he could redeem his acts, forgive himself and return to the Pack, any pack. Nathan's words put an end to that hope.

"You're making me outcast."

"I'm sorry. I truly am, but the needs of the pack must come before everything."

"And I suppose this goes for Antonia, too, and the other wolves we managed to rescue."

"As of now, the gates are closed to outsiders. All packs have orders to detain new wolves on sight. We can't take the chance. If what your vampire says is true, then a war is about to start, and I, for one, won't be giving the vampires an advantage or a foot in the door."

"So does this mean you won't give us any manpower to stop this war before it starts?"

"Sorry, but you're on your own."

"I can't believe you're turning your back on this."

"I'm not. I'm doing what's best for the majority, and from where I'm sitting, so far it looks like this is a vampire power struggle. I say let the bloodsuckers fight it out."

"And if the wrong side wins and comes after your pack next?"

"Then we fight."

"Aren't you worried the humans will notice if

vampires and wolves start attacking each other?"

Nathan didn't reply.

A low whistle left Marc's lips. "I don't fucking believe it. You're hoping for war."

"Not hoping but not hiding from it either. The vampires struck first when they changed my father and then let him come after us. Now, they think to screw with us again by having us fight in their struggle for who gets power. Enough is enough. The world is changing. The old ways aren't working anymore. Pack Laws need to be rewritten, and perhaps it's time our role in the world changes, too."

"What if your plan backfires? What if humans don't take the news of your existence well and decide to hunt you?"

Nathan laughed, but there was nothing mirthful about it. "We've hidden before; we could hide again. Or not. I will promise that we won't go looking for trouble, but if the vampires come after us, we won't run, and they will die."

With a *click*, the line went dead, and Marc spent a moment staring in dumbfounded astonishment at the phone.

"Nathan is an idiot," Toni muttered.

"Nathan is a leader in a tough predicament," Thaddeus added. "He's right, the needs of his pack must come first, but it's a shame he'd rather risk all their lives because of his pride than sacrifice a possible few and help me to nip this in the bud."

Would Nathan's help really make a difference though? Marc couldn't help but wonder. "He's got a point, though, about things needing to change. I don't agree war or fighting is the best way, but the world is a different place. The pack rules are long overdue for an overhaul."

"I can think of one law in particular," Toni chimed in.

"But change is one thing, and announcing our presence to the world another," Thaddeus argued. "The humans aren't going to accept either of our races with open arms. We're predators."

"But we don't feed on humans," Marc interjected.

"You don't. Nathan's pack doesn't, but can we say the same of the wolves in Morpheus's care? Who's to say he won't keep a few to get the massacre started?"

Marc almost said that was too sick even for a vampire to plot but held his tongue. Just because Thad was proving to be a decent sort didn't mean the rest of the vampires were. Actually, according to Thad, he was in the minority. *Just fucking great. I'm siding with the underdogs.*

"You know, when you say shit like that, I've really got to wonder why the fuck I hang around," Marc muttered.

"Because you and Thaddeus might not like to admit it, but you're both good guys."

He and the vampire exchanged a glance.

"Good?" Thaddeus practically choked on the word.

"Is she doing this on purpose, do you think?"

Marc asked.

"What's wrong with me calling you guys heroes?"

"You'll ruin my reputation," Thad growled. "We can't have that. Come, wolf, time we taught our female just how bad we are."

As one they rose and carted a giggling Toni off to bed. It didn't take them long for her to gasp—naked, writhing, and gleaming with desire—that they were bad. Oh so very, deliciously bad.

Chapter Twenty-Eight

An hour or so later, they were on the road, the vehicle they borrowed not exactly luxurious, but the pickup truck in the garage, with the plow hooked to the front was less noticeable than Thaddeus's car with the torn hood and roof. Marc drove this leg of the trip, with Toni seated in the middle and Thaddeus on the other side. Cozy, but surprisingly pleasant.

Thaddeus was still trying to come to terms with the speed at which his immortal life had changed. He'd gone from a boring and dull existence, where his primary amusement was stalking miscreants and taunting Morpheus, to embarking on a quest to save his kind, stop a war, oh, and get romantically involved with a woman and another man. Or at least the woman. The fact that she came with a hairy attachment he had yet to kill was something he still couldn't quite comprehend. *I have never been one to keep pets.*

In times past, Thaddeus would have easily solved the dilemma by snapping a neck and claiming her for his own. He had no interest in Marc as a lover, a snack perhaps but nothing beyond that. However, Thaddeus couldn't deny the enjoyment they'd partaken of the previous night. Watching Toni's climax at the hands and cock of another added a certain erotic element Thaddeus had never expected.

Also unexpected was his urge to not just lay a claim to his lovely Latina but to somehow mark the wolf, to forge a true three-way bond between them. It wasn't as if it were unheard of. Many vampires chose to align their immortal lives with several humans, the need for blood being one reason, trustworthy companionship another. The concept of doing it with Lycans, though? That was unheard of. Their kind weren't supposed to mix. A whole mortal enemies blah, blah, blah thing passed down through the generations. And yet, it wasn't because they weren't compatible. Wolves weren't toxic to vampires. On the contrary, rumor held they were quite delicious. And here he had two to choose from. Just thinking about the rich feast if he could call them both his own…the warm fluid, flowing salty and fresh from the flesh. The pulsing of the vein. The beat of their hearts. The…

Hunger had to be to blame for these crazy thoughts. *Bite the dog, indeed.* Yet, despite his inner chastisement, he couldn't completely banish the idea.

The miles flew by, as did the hours. The compound was a six-hour drive if they kept close to the speed limits and didn't stop for longer than it took to fill a tank with gas. Still, they'd be cutting it close, their erotic interlude with Toni having burned a portion of their night time.

As they neared the ranch, Thad checked in with Sasha by phone. "Have you arrived?" he asked without greeting.

"And a hello to you too, boss. Yes, I'm here with the gang, plus four new members. You'll be glad to know they're house broken, if frisky and distrustful."

A masculine "Watch the insults, shorty" followed her announcement. A scuffle and a grunt soon followed.

"Are they behaving?"

"Nothing I can't handle."

Thad smiled. If the wolves thought to mess with Sasha, they'd find she could give as good as she got. "Any signs of ghouls or outsiders?"

"Coast is clear."

A good sign, or so he hoped. While the compound was built to withstand an assault, he'd prefer not to have it tested until he was within its confines. "What of our guests? Could you tell if their minds were tampered with?"

"Well, they're not raving lunatics if that's what you're asking."

"It's not, and you know it."

Sasha sighed. "I know, but as you know, my mind tricks aren't that strong. I did try to compel them. It didn't work."

"What of the others I sent with you; Jorge, Pierrot, Anabel, and Tim. Did they try?" Four other vampires he'd picked up over the years who owed him their lives and loyalty.

"Also no luck. Either these guys are mentally strong, or we were too late and they're fucking with us." And if they were, Sasha would show no mercy.

"We'll know soon enough. I'll be arriving within the hour."

"I'll roll out the red carpet for your arrival."

"Smartass. I don't know why I don't kill you for your impertinence."

"Because then you'd have no one left who doesn't fear your mighty scowl."

Wrong. He now had Toni and Marc who treated him like he was…normal. Was that their appeal? That they didn't fear him? Or cower? Maybe, and yet he'd never wanted anything more with Sasha. How interesting.

"Yoohoo, minion paging her boss, can you hear me?"

"What is it? I hit a dead spot," he lied.

"I wanted to know if I should arm our newest recruits or not."

In other words, did they trust they'd gotten to them in time, or should they worry that they were Trojan wolves? "Not. I'll be there soon and will let you know if they've been tampered with. In the meantime, if you are attacked, they have their wolf sides they can rely on. Stay close to the house, and don't let them out of your sight."

He disconnected and drummed his fingers on the side panel of the door, watching, with unseeing eyes, the shadowed scenery as it flashed by.

"Penny for your thoughts?" Toni murmured.

"I'd prefer a kiss."

She leaned over and pecked him on the cheek, a noisy, wet smack that had him grimacing. "That was not what I was hoping for."

"I know, but the look on your face was worth it," she replied with a giggle. "So, what's got you looking like death warmed over?"

Marc snickered.

Thaddeus shot them a dark look. She smirked while Marc kept his eyes on the road, only a curve to his lips betraying his amusement.

No respect, and yet it didn't irritate him, judging by his answering smile. "In case you didn't eavesdrop, Sasha managed to acquire four of the rogues."

"Yeah, I kind of couldn't help but overhear. So she's got four of them at this place we're heading to, but there's a question about whether or not another vampire got to them first."

"Exactly."

"How exactly can you tell if they've been whammied?" Marc asked.

"Simple, really. I try to compel them myself."

"So you can't compel someone who's already compelled?" Toni asked with a crease between her brows.

"Yes and no. A weak compulsion can shatter under a strong one. When we get to the compound, I shall interview them one by one. I'll find the truth."

"Or not. What if the other guy is better at the whole mind-control thing than you?"

He straightened in his seat. "Doubtful. I am considered the strongest in that art."

"Or so you think. What if they make you think you've got them as your minion, when, in reality, you don't?"

"My power is stronger than Morpheus's."

"But what if it wasn't Morpheus who got to them but this mysterious new player we've yet to meet? The one the witch told us about."

It was Thaddeus's turn to frown. That had not occurred to him. The wolf did make a good point—give the dog a bone. He should temper his overconfidence, lest it lead him into making a fatal mistake. "I'd say it is unlikely but something I cannot ignore."

Toni pressed closer to him, as if seeking reassurance. "If we err on the side of caution, then how do we know if we can trust them?"

Marc gave him the solution. "Feed them some of Roderick's ashes."

Simple. And, as far as Thaddeus could tell, effective. "You know that's not a bad idea. We have enough left to do that, but then the dilemma is what to do with—"

Whatever he meant to say got lost in the loud pops of tires exploding and then the scream of rubber as the truck skidded sideways. Marc battled for control of the vehicle, but with the tires blown combined with the speed they traveled? It was a lost cause.

It didn't take Thaddeus's tingle of danger to know they were in trouble. Someone had set a trap, and they'd driven right into it.

The truck tilted, wobbled, then rolled, tossing them around like rag dolls, the older vehicle not having the safety features of a newer vehicle. In other words, broken seat belts and no airbags.

The truck rolled to a stop, thankfully upright. Phone still in hand, Thaddeus sent a quick text message to Sasha.

Attacked. Engage lockdown mode.

Hopefully Sasha would get herself and the others into the house and enable the protective system before something befell them. As for Toni, Marc, and himself, it seemed they'd have to put their fighting skills to the test. *And with me still hungry.* He now regretted not taking Toni's blood earlier. He could have laid her hesitation to rest, shown her the pleasure to be had in giving blood.

But no, he had to get all weak and sentimental. Idiot. He hoped he didn't pay for his folly with his life because he doubted by the stench wafting through the broken windows that he'd find sustenance in this battle.

A shame. Nothing freaked a mortal enemy out more than when you ate his comrade before his wide, white eyes and promised it would be his turn next.

While the truck had come to rest on its wheels, a final flip leaving them upright, it didn't mean they'd emerged completely unscathed. Thaddeus ignored his various contusions and the few cuts. They'd heal soon enough, especially once he ate. Of more concern were his companions. Toni groaned, alive, but concussed he'd wager, judging by her fluttering lids and waxen complexion. As for Marc, a male who'd been knocked around a time or two in his life, he shook off the stupor with a, "Fuck me, that was a trip. What happened?"

"Ambush," Thaddeus stated unnecessarily.

To his credit, the wolf didn't panic or show fear. On the contrary, he went into alert mode, head swinging as he took in the darkness surrounding them, seeking out the approaching enemy. There were quite a few to choose from.

"I'll take the half-dozen to the left. You take the half-dozen to the right. Loser has to watch." Challenge tossed, Marc winked before hoisting himself out the window.

Thaddeus sat stunned for a moment then laughed. Damn it all if he wasn't liking the damned wolf more and more. Watch indeed. "Stay here. We'll take care of this," he told Toni, who bled from a gash on her temple and still couldn't focus her eyes. The coppery scent proved too much. He couldn't resist leaning over for a lick—for good luck, of course. *Mmmm.*

Before he could get distracted by the tempting feast, he dove out his own window only a moment before a body lunged at it. He narrowly avoided the claws, but his midair contortion saw him hit the ground in a less-than-graceful roll.

Bouncing to his feet, he managed to raise an arm and block the swipe from the attacking ghoul. And what a prize his opponent was; unshaven, unbathed, his eyes a feral red and his canines an unhealthy yellow. Thaddeus began to see why Nathan wouldn't exert himself to save these Lycan dregs of society. He knew what his first impulse was.

Crack. The neck snapped as he twisted it sharply. The body dropped to the ground, temporarily incapacitated, but Thaddeus didn't have time to worry about it. A more permanent death would have to wait because the enemy chose to rush him, and he was engaged in a battle for his life.

Thaddeus considered himself a great fighter. He'd had years after all to fine-tune his skills, not to mention he'd absorbed the memories and experience of countless vampires. But even the most battle hardened couldn't hope to prevail against stupid odds.

For every lunge he parried, a swipe left a gash. For every gash that he avoided, a punch knocked him back. Adrenaline coursed through every inch of him as he moved in a blur, a berserker-type rage settling over him, allowing him to move without thought, to tear and rip into his enemies savagely.

Things weren't looking so good, not for him or his companions. But he couldn't give up, not so long as his heart beat, which unfortunately didn't seem like it would for much longer.

How ironic death is coming for me, just when I was starting to enjoy life again.

Chapter Twenty-Nine

Marc had only seconds to call upon his wolf, which meant bye-bye to yet another set of clothes. However, if he managed to get out of this ambush naked but alive, he'd count himself lucky. His initial estimate of half a dozen to the left proved accurate, but not so for the right. Marc only had a moment to realize Thad was going to get swarmed before his first ghoul attacked.

Knowing what to expect this time, he didn't waste time grappling; he went for weak spots. Throat if he could reach it to tear it out. A close second was the legs. If they couldn't walk, it made them less of a threat.

His strategy proved effective. While ghouls twitched on the ground and reached for him, he managed to keep to his four furry feet and cause some damage, enough that he felt the need to leave his group of ghouls and head to help Thaddeus, who was practically buried in them.

He had to hand it to the old bloodsucker though. Thaddeus wasn't going down without a hell of a fight. Partway there, Marc stumbled as he heard Toni yell, "Let me go!"

Pivoting, he shot a glance in the direction of the truck. A ghoul who'd decided to skip the main battle was pulling his woman from the cab. She didn't go willingly. Toni thrashed and kicked and flailed, but for some reason, she didn't let her wolf rise.

What was she thinking? As a human she was helpless.

Marc's fear for her gave him adrenaline as he sprinted in their direction. Lucky for her, or not, the monster didn't seem interested in tearing her apart. On the contrary, the ghoul dragged Toni to a dark figure standing just outside the fight zone. Marc didn't need a good sense of smell to know this was a vampire, probably the one in charge of the show.

Toni must have recognized the threat of the silent figure, too, because even over the sounds of the skirmish, he heard her horrified, "No, not again."

Marc poured on the speed, his four feet fleet but not fast enough to reach her before the vampire laid his hand on her head and forced her to meet his stare.

She ate the ashes. She's immune. She's…

Marc stumbled as Toni fell over sideways, not dead; no, the link between them reassured him she lived, but ashes or not, she had succumbed to the vampire.

But he can't have her. No way was he letting that bastard take his Toni. Marc wouldn't allow her to suffer again. He renewed his efforts to reach her, dodging the few ghouls between him and the vampire.

He tried to ignore the insidious whispers in his mind. *Weakling. Do you really think you can take on a master vampire?*

I didn't succumb to Thad.

Neither did Toni, but she fell before this new player. Who's to say you won't too? Are you ready to become a slave again?

The fear of not controlling his own mind made him want to turn around, tuck his tail, and take off for parts unknown. Oh, how the cowardly route beckoned. But Marc didn't give in to his fear. Toni needed him. He needed to do this, needed to prove to himself that he had the inner strength to prevail.

I'm better than I was. Stronger. I can do this. He would do this.

The ghoul who'd brought Toni to the vampire turned to face him. Its bloodless lips split into an evil smile. The red glint in its eyes sent a shiver through Marc, but he didn't stop his mad rush.

The ghoul ran to meet him, and they collided in a tangle of limbs, fur, and teeth. Snapping and growling, he bit anything he could clamp his jaws around, tearing hunks of flesh. His earlier finesse fled in his frenzied need to rescue Toni.

Chaotic or not, his crazy attack did the job. Head hanging lopsided, its arms broken, the monster fell to the ground and thrashed ineffectively.

Facing the unknown vampire, muzzle coated in dark fluid, his eyes surely glowing with a yellow fire, Marc advanced with a growl.

"Foolish dog," mocked the stranger. "Do you really think you can take me on?"

Marc bared even more teeth as he slunk forward.

"As if I'd sully myself fighting a mere canine."

With a snarl that turned into a bellow, and a rearranging of limbs, his body switched the quickest he'd ever managed. Marc stood and faced the vampire. "If you won't face my wolf, then how about man to man? Or are you too chicken?"

"Such confidence from one who was previously a puppet. Tell me, dog, how would you like to serve a new master?" Red eyes bored into his. Oily tendrils probed at his mind. Sick fear coated Marc's tongue as the icy remembrance of his past came back to haunt him.

Not again. He imagined a wall around his mind with a great big fucking no-trespassing sign. Bit by bit, his confidence melted the trepidation as the mind pokes hit the barrier and were stopped.

The vampire couldn't control him. Marc feigned a yawn. "Been there. Done that. Not doing it again."

Bloodless lips tightened as the vampire realized his mind games wouldn't work. "You might be enthralled to Thaddeus, but once he dies, your mind will be ripe for the picking."

So this vampire didn't know of the power of Roderick's ashes. Good. Marc wasn't about to enlighten him. "What makes you think you're strong enough?"

"I am Morpheus."

"Never heard of you." Marc lied and enjoyed the annoyance on the bloodsucker's face.

"Remember my name, dog, because, soon, you will revere it and me because I will lead the world into a new age. A dark age. A bloody—"

"Cut the crap. I'm not interested. Why not give up the mind games and fight like a real man, or have you forgotten how?" With clenched fists, Marc took a menacing step forward.

"I have a more interesting idea. How would you fare against one you cared for?"

What did he mean?

Morpheus smiled, revealing yellowed teeth. "Attack, my newest bitch. Let's see how your lover feels about snapping your pretty little neck."

Crouched at Morpheus's feet, Toni raised her disheveled head. Her eyes glinted yellow, a sign of the wolf behind them. Her lips pulled back over teeth, a wild, yet feral smile. Then she lunged.

Chapter Thirty

Despite the knock to her head, Toni understood they were in deep shit. Just one problem, she was too muddled to do anything about it. Through the ringing in her ears, she vaguely heard the word ambush and Thad's admonition to stay in the truck. Thing was staying in the truck wasn't a guarantee of protection. Evil lurked outside, and she could feel the nudge of it at the edge of her mind.

Knock, knock. Who wants in?

It wasn't Thaddeus. She knew his touch; it was gentle and not creepy. This mind probe reminded her more of Roderick's methods. Like a battering ram coated in slime. Someone on the impromptu battleground was trying to take over her mind. But who?

Taking in deep breaths, she managed to calm the spinning in her head, enough so she could open her eyes without wanting to throw up. She wanted to shut them just as quickly.

Chaos met her gaze. Despite the darkness, the one remaining headlight on the truck lit the surrounding area enough for her to see a nasty fight occurring. On the one side, she caught the blur of russet fur as Marc darted in and out among a group of ghouls, never standing still for long, just grabbing a chunk of whatever he could reach and yanking.

Gross, and yet her wolf heartily approved of his methods.

It also appeared as if he wasn't in too much trouble, but Thaddeus on the other hand…He wasn't faring as well. It seemed the bulk of the attack was geared toward him. She could barely see him for the bodies, some prone but a large number still upright, trying to take him down.

Through their bond, she could feel his fatigue, and she cursed herself for not having had the courage to feed him. Here he fought for his life, but without the strength he should have had. *Could have had if I'd not been so damned squeamish.*

That would change if they made it out of this mess alive. Lots of things would change. But first, she needed to help turn the tides.

Thad might have ordered her to stay in the truck, but now that the initial disorientation from the crash had worn off, she needed to act. She wouldn't sit waiting to see who would emerge victor, not when she could make a difference.

Her wolf, pacing the confines of her mind, agreed. *Hunt. Kill.*

But were her skills best used on the field of battle or elsewhere? The vampire who'd yet to show himself still prodded at her mental walls. He was the driving force behind this attack. If they removed him, would the ghouls falter? What should she do? Help Thad or go after the vampire?

The decision was taken out of her hands as the door to the truck ripped open with a scream of metal. The ghoul who'd decided to invite her to the party caught her by the arm and yanked her out.

Immediately, her wolf clamored to escape. Toni fought the snarl itching to escape and the beast within. *Not yet.* She needed to keep her wits and find the other vampire, the one testing her walls, the one running this freak show.

When the ghoul dragged her instead of trying to eat her, Toni put on a good show, fighting and kicking, yelling and cursing.

Her theatrics stopped when they reached the dark stranger who stood apart from the battle. Forced to her knees, she could only whisper, "Not again," as she stared into his soulless red eyes.

The slimy touch came again. The hell-lit eyes bored into hers, and her lips went slack, her eyes unfocused.

Obey, he commanded.

She knelt on the ground and watched as Thad went down under a swath of bodies. Watched as Marc came barreling to her rescue, teeth bared, desperate to save her.

And when the command came, ordering her to attack, she couldn't hold back. Couldn't stop…she lunged.

Parts of her wolf sprouted; her jaw cracked as it elongated and her teeth dropped. Her fingers cramped, and she screamed while howling as her claws sprang forth. Caught in a half-shift, she did as the vampire commanded, but on her own terms.

She thrust up, jabbing her clawed mutant hand

into the vampire's stomach. She muttered in a guttural voice, "Surprise, asshole!" before sinking her teeth into the bared throat of her enemy. She closed her eyes to avoid seeing the spurting blood but couldn't help the exultation as she tore into the one who thought he would control her.

Never again. Never again will I be a victim.

The vampire she savaged fell to the ground, but she didn't release her grip. She knew how tricky they were, how hard to kill. Besides, her wolf enjoyed herself. Even if only half shifted, she reveled in their power, their strength. The kill. Warm liquid coated her tongue. Adrenaline coursed through her body. *Die, you bastard.*

Arms, human ones with a scent she well recognized, wrapped around her from behind.

"It's over, Toni," Marc murmured. "You can let go now."

She growled and shook her head from side to side, further tearing at the body. Vampires could regenerate. She had to make sure it stayed dead.

Her mate, the one who had yet to mark her, tore her away from her prey. She broke free of his hold and landed on her knees and hands. Her claws dug into the soft ground, and a rumble preceded the lift of her lip over teeth. The coppery tang of blood on her tongue was swallowed, the first of many mouthfuls as she imbibed of her enemy's lifeblood.

"Toni." Her mate knelt before her wearing his skin. He held out his hands and spoke words she understood but did not want to heed. "He's dead,

Toni. You did it. You killed the vampire."

But what of his minions? The ones who smelled wrong? She swung her head and saw the pile of bodies. Yet, she didn't see or scent her other mate. She whined.

Her wolf mate frowned. "What's wrong? Are you injured?"

Where had her other mate gone? The one she also planned to mark and keep. She peered at the darkness and sniffed at the air. She caught the wide eyes of her wolf mate and saw his mouth open to speak. She whirled and caught the vampire, head lolling sickly, teeth bared in a hiss as he lunged at her with a dagger. The cheater.

But he never reached her. A fist punched through the upper body and emerged holding a beating heart.

Eyes wide, the one known as Morpheus, hissed, "This is not over. My master will avenge me."

She barked, ready to attack, but the vampire, now truly dead, slumped to the ground, revealing her other mate, battered but alive, holding the organ he'd stolen.

Like a true predator, her mate took a bite, a big one, and said, in words her other self understood, "I don't know about you guys, but I worked up quite the appetite."

Chapter Thirty-One

Okay, perhaps offering the warm heart to his comrades was perhaps not the sanest thing he'd ever done, but in Thaddeus's defense, it was considered quite the compliment in the vampire world, as it meant he was willing to share his power.

With grimaces of distaste, Toni and Marc declined. Their loss. With a shrug, Thaddeus finished his treat, feeling his strength return and his wounds healing. Nothing like partaking of a master vampire's warm heart to give a boost to a weakened body.

The skies chose that moment to release their moist bounty, a cool, fresh rain pelting them and cleansing the blood from their skin. But even clean, Thaddeus stood apart, watching as Marc held a shuddering Toni, a woman who'd unleashed her savage side and watched him eat another man's heart. *What does she think of me now?*

Thaddeus wouldn't make excuses for what he was. He was a vampire. Eating the flesh of his enemies was a part of his life. A need. Although, in this case, he could have done without some of Morpheus's warped memories, memories he'd have to sift through later when he had the time to look for clues.

Accepting who he was, though, didn't prevent

him from feeling a pang at Toni's rejection of him. It seemed he was too much of a monster for her. He turned away only to hear her whisper, "Thad?"

Her fear and doubt touched him, but more astonishing, a glimmer of affection tickled him too. He whirled back.

Standing in the cradle of Marc's arms, she faced him with big eyes, her hands held out to him. Calling him.

He didn't hesitate. In a blink he stood before her, and she threw herself at him, her arms wrapping around him in a tight hug. "I thought you were dead," she whispered, her voice choked with emotion.

"You give me too little credit. I'll admit the odds weren't favorable, and yet, Marc wagered me, and anyone who knows me will attest I hate to lose a bet."

She sniffled and peered at him through eyes wet with tears and raindrops. "Bet? What bet?"

"One you will enjoy, I assure you."

"Technically, I won," Marc boasted, completing their circle by hugging Toni from behind.

"Only because you had less of the enemy to fight."

"Not my fault they chose to pick on you."

Toni made a noise. "Are you both seriously bickering right now? We just fought off an army of ghouls and killed a vampire."

"She's right," Thaddeus announced. "This isn't a time for petty squabbles but a time to celebrate."

That said, he gave in to temptation and kissed Toni's lips, tasting the salt of her tears.

Her lips immediately parted for him, her soft breath warming him with her life. Her taste roused his hungers, the erotic one and the one that ached to taste her blood again, to lay claim to her, lest another try to steal her.

I will make her mine.

He wasn't the only one determined to stake a claim. Marc nuzzled at her neck, nipping and lapping at her skin. How lovely she would look when she wore their marks, one on each side of her tanned neck, one that showed the world this woman was protected—and loved.

Because there was no doubting it. Thaddeus loved Toni. Loved her with an inconceivable passion despite their short acquaintance.

A love he would cherish and protect even against the future threats facing them. A passion he would have to fulfill later when he got rid of his audience that let out a low whistle.

"Holy shit, boss. You weren't kidding when you said you got ambushed." Sasha arrived without any noise of warning, or was it the blood roaring through him, making his heart pound, that rendered him deaf?

Marc sighed as he leaned his chin on Toni's shoulder. "Your lackey has awful timing."

"Or not," Thaddeus remarked. "Observe. Keys." He held out his hand.

Sasha quirked a brow. "Excuse me?"

"I highly doubt you ran the ten miles from the compound to here, which means you parked up the road. I need your vehicle."

"And how will I get back?" she grumbled as she handed them over.

"Don't tell me you came alone."

"No. They're just not as quick," she replied sassily as several other vampires materialized behind her.

"Catch a ride back with them after you take care of the bodies. I want nothing left of Morpheus. And I mean nothing." He arched a brow, and Sasha grimaced.

"You know it's raining, right?"

"Yes."

"Ugh. And me who likes her steak well done," she grumbled. "I'll take care of the mess."

"Where are the wolves?"

Sasha grinned. "Sleeping. As soon as I read the word ambush, I tranquilized them, just in case, and locked them in the panic room. A girl can't be too safe."

"Excellent. I don't want to be disturbed for the next twenty-four hours unless we're under attack."

"Only twenty-four?"

"You're right. Make it two days."

Toni gasped, and Marc chuckled.

With danger averted, Thaddeus wouldn't waste time. Who knew when the next calamity would strike? He intended to be bonded before that happened. Oh, and fed…well fed, both sexually and otherwise.

Chapter Thirty-Two

Thad drove the last leg to the compound in their borrowed car. A two-seat sports car, which meant Toni got to sit on Marc's lap. His naked lap. His naked lap with an erect cock poking at her backside.

Something about prevailing against death and danger was arousing. Stimulating. Having a wet woman, whose scent drove him wild, who kept wiggling deliciously and casting him sultry glances, just added fuel to the fire stoking him.

Thad must have felt some of the simmering energy because his fingers danced along her thigh, skirting the vee between her thighs and causing Toni's breath to catch.

They couldn't get to the compound fast enough.

Oddly enough, Toni, her voice breathy and soft, spoke in the erotically charged silence. "That was pretty intense back there."

"If you mean fucking scary, then, yeah," Marc noted. He wasn't too macho to admit he'd feared. Especially for her. *And there was a moment where I wondered if I'd end up a vampire puppet again.* Thankfully, he'd prevailed.

"I want to thank you for not turning away from me even after seeing me as I am," Thad added without his usual sarcasm, his voice low and solemn.

"You're a vampire. And I'm a wolf. I'll admit,

the gorier aspects to our identities still make me squeamish, but hiding from them or pretending they don't exist isn't an option. I am who I am. Just like you both are who you are. If I'm going to have you in my lives, then I guess I'll have to accept that."

"Does that mean you're ready to bond with us?" The question slipped from Marc, but once out in the open, it hung there, begging for an answer.

He didn't have to wait long.

Toni stroked his cheek, tenderness in her touch. "Yes. If there's one thing I've learned, it's life is too short and unpredictable to hesitate over risks. I want you. Both of you. In my life. My bed. And my heart. That is, if you both still want me."

"Of course I do," Marc exclaimed. "Haven't you figured out yet that I'm howling mad about you?"

"And I love you as well, little wolf," Thaddeus murmured, somehow managing to drive with his head turned. "You've brought meaning back into my life. You and, much as it surprises me to admit, Marc. I would bind myself not only to you but also to him. If he is willing? It has been a long time since I've met a male I'd be willing to call friend." Dark eyes met Marc's blue ones.

The admission startled Marc. He'd not really thought of Thaddeus in terms of claiming. Usually in a pack, the males claimed the female, and the others just learned to live with or beat the hell out of each other.

What Thaddeus seemed to suggest was an additional bond, one that would also tie them as more than friends. "Before I say yes, does this involve any kinky shit? Because I'll admit, while I admire and covet Toni's ass, yours, not so much."

Thaddeus laughed. "The tie I speak of is one of blood. A bite exchange where I inject you with some of my essence. It will link us and allow us to share some of our thoughts and feelings. It will protect you against my kind as well."

"Will you let me bite you back? Fair is fair," Marc countered, not sure why he asked, other than his wolf seemed to not like the idea of it being a one-way chomp.

The request took Thaddeus by surprise judging by the expression on his face, and he pulled into a circular drive and parked before a brightly lit ranch house before replying. "I've never considered before letting another mark me. And I'm going to assume by Toni's avid interest in my answer that your wolf desires a nip of my flesh, too?"

She nodded.

Thaddeus looked away from them for a moment, thoughtful, silent. When he did finally face them again, he gave a sharp nod. "I've never heard of a wolf marking a vampire. Then again, Lycans usually don't get involved with my kind unless it's in a match to the death. But as we've proven, our species are compatible, or at least we are. This entire adventure has been new and unheard of. Why shouldn't our claiming be as well?" He shook his head and grinned wryly. "And here I thought I'd seen it all. I guess there are still things to discover even when one has lived as long as I. Now that it's been decided, shall we adjourn to my quarters before the dawning sun lays waste to our plans? I'd prefer not to get roasted just as we've come to an agreement that is satisfactory to us all."

"You and your fancy talk," Marc snorted. "Why not say it like it is? You're horny and hungry, and you want some loving before you pass out snoring."

Only a slight twitch of Thad's lips betrayed his amusement. "Crass, but to the point. Yes, I would have us join in pleasurable pursuits, a fitting end for a trying, yet victorious day. If you'll follow me."

Thaddeus led the way into the sprawling ranch house, but Marc paid scarce attention to the decor or the details. How could he when Toni nibbled at his neck, her plush body cradled in his arms because he'd chosen to carry her?

A set of double doors, carved white nine-foot panels, gave entry to a sumptuous suite done in a light blue and gray that he wouldn't have attributed to a vampire. But then again, Thaddeus wasn't anything like the stereotypes. The massive bedroom had an en suite bathroom with a shower big enough for numerous people. Not that he cared. Warm water and soap were his primary objective, both needed to fully cleanse them of the remaining filth from the battle, as well as to heat Toni's clammy, rain-soaked skin.

It didn't take long to strip the rags from Thad and Toni and huddle under the hot spray shooting from the dozens of showerheads.

Thaddeus and Marc each took a sponge in hand and took to lathering Toni from head to toe, ignoring her husky laughter and claim she could care for herself. She could. She'd proven that, but this wasn't about caring for her so much as reassuring himself that she was whole. Safe. *Mine*. And Thad's.

Could he really go through with a bite exchange with the vampire? Bind himself to a bloodsucker for life? A man who called him friend? A man who would love and protect Toni as much as him? *He might not be pack, but he's offering me a chance to belong. A new sort of dysfunctional family.* Which was more than he'd had several days ago. Why the fuck not?

He met the vampire's eyes over the head of their woman. "I say you and I get this over with."

"Afraid you'll get cold feet, wolf?" Thad mocked.

"No. Okay, maybe a little. No offense but the idea of another guy biting me is kind of weird."

"Would it help if I let you choose the spot?"

"You mean it doesn't have to be the neck?"

Thad chuckled. "No. What do you say we exchange marks on the forearm? Then we can display them easily if needed, without them being blatant."

"Sounds good."

They eyed each other, neither making the first move. Toni sighed and shook her head. "Oh, for God's sake. Give me your hands." Tugging their extended arms, Toni arranged them on either side of her, a naked buffer between their bodies but leaving them almost eye to eye over her shorter frame.

Arms draped around her shoulders, it proved easy with his free hand to grasp Thad's extended limb. Thad did likewise. They held them up, lips a hairsbreadth from flesh, eyes locked.

"On the count of three," Marc said. "One, two—"

Before he could tense and say three, Thad bit down, hard, and Marc reacted by chomping down.

Skin broke, blood flowed. The coppery fluid hit his tongue, and he swallowed, his gaze still locked with Thad's.

The shock of their joining hit him like a tidal wave. Thoughts, emotions, even memories slammed him in a whirlwind moment. He glimpsed Thad's violence, triumphs, tribulations, his loneliness, and then his joy as he found somewhere, make that someone, to belong to. It was overwhelming, deeply personal, too much. Too…pleasurable?

The crazy chaos of their joining turned to bliss as, with soft tugs, Thad drank from him, pulling his essence. Marc's cock, which had deflated with trepidation, swelled and pressed against Toni's lower belly.

Fuck me, that feels good. If this feels great, then imagine if he fed while I was balls-deep in Toni. He couldn't help but moan at the sensuous thought, something they'd definitely have to try in the future.

All too soon, Thad released him, licking the wound and stopping the sluggish flow of blood.

"It is done," he stated unnecessarily.

"Maybe you guys are, but this girl is far from finished," Toni quipped.

"I think little wolf is complaining we're neglecting her."

"I say we do something about it." Marc grabbed a wet and slippery Toni and tossed her over his shoulder. She squealed and laughed as he carried her out to the bedroom and tossed her onto the bed, where she bounced before coming to rest in a sensually splayed heap.

"I'm soaking the sheets."

"Not yet, but you will be," Marc promised as he advanced on her. He'd waited long enough. Time to claim his woman. A movement by his side made him revise that. *Our woman.*

Chapter Thirty-Three

If someone would have told Toni watching two guys bite each other with her sandwiched between them would be one of the most intense moments of her life, she would have scoffed. But even though neither of them had bitten her, she caught some of the backlash from their joining. She couldn't help but bask in the warmth of knowing they did it not just for themselves but for her. To be with her. Because they loved her.

And to think I wondered why any woman would agree to more than one lover.

Toni was more than ready to let them claim her. She wanted to join them and belong to them and have them belong to her. Not because of any laws or protection, but because she wanted them. She loved them.

I want them to be mine.

Marc might have thought to tease her or shock her with his words of making her wetter, as if that could happen. Her pussy had never hummed so strongly or felt so slick. She crooked a finger, beckoning to them both. On to the bed they came, on their knees before her, erect cocks jutting proudly from their bodies.

She pursed her lips in invitation and was rewarded with a kiss from Thad that left them both panting in moments, probably because she'd also grabbed his throbbing penis and stroked it, but he wasn't the only one in need of attention. She ended the kiss with Thad and tilted her head to the side to offer her mouth to Marc. He kissed her hard, his tongue jabbing between her lips as he slid his hand up her thigh, tickling and teasing.

A moan was swallowed by his mouth when Thad found her clit and rubbed it, circling her swollen nub with the tip of his finger, distracting her. They pushed her down onto the bed until she lay flat, with one of them on either side, stroking, touching, kissing. Two fingers, one from each of her lovers, circled the entrance of her sex. She couldn't help but squirm, needing more.

Instead they stopped. She opened her eyes and made a sound of protest. "Dying over here."

"Hold her," Thad ordered. "I'm feeling a need for some honey."

Marc tossed her a wicked smile as he pulled her arms above her head, his grip strong and unrelenting. She gazed at him through slitted eyes, passion making her lids heavy. She felt more than saw Thad kneeling between her thighs. Up went her legs, pushed open and apart, exposing her to his gaze, but not for long.

A wet tongue stroked her silken slit, lapping at her juices, giving her such pleasure that she arched, her body reacting. They pushed her back down and held her flat, a willing victim to their sensual torture of her body.

Face buried against her sex, Thad lapped from her and made contented sounds, sounds that rumbled against her and served to raise her excitement. Toni panted into Marc's mouth, distracted and floating on an erotic cloud as the exquisite strokes of Thad's tongue drove her ever upward to the pinnacle of ultimate pleasure.

Too quick. She wanted to hold on to this incredible moment, to prolong the pleasure, but when Marc shifted his attention from her mouth and latched onto a tight nipple, it proved too much.

She exploded with a scream, but one orgasm wasn't enough. The waves of her climax slowed to a shuddering ripple, and yet her body still felt like a wire strung too tight. One that wouldn't take much to snap again.

And they seemed intent on making it happen.

Marc bit down on her nipple, not hard enough to hurt or break skin but enough to send a pleasurable jolt down to her pussy. Thad caught the clench of her sex on his still busy tongue.

"Enough," she gasped. "You're going to kill me."

"We can't have that," Thad purred against her nether lips, the soft susurration of his breath enough to make her sensitized sex shiver.

"I think she's ready," Marc growled. "I know I am."

It took only a slight shuffle, their capable hands doing all the work to position her so she found herself astride Marc, Thad's hands on her waist holding her above Marc's thick penis, which prodded at the entrance to her sex.

She placed her hands on his chest, leaning slightly forward, her hair whispering over her shoulders to tease the tips of her breasts. Slowly, Thad eased her down, controlling her descent as she took Marc into her pussy. How was it possible for him to be wider than before? Her breathing hitched as her pussy clenched, making it even tighter.

Marc's eyes closed, and the muscles in his neck corded as if he fought the pleasure. "Too tight," he gasped. "Fuck me, that feels good."

How powerful she felt in that moment knowing how she affected him. She didn't wait for Thad to continue his slow descent. With a wiggle of her hips, she slammed down on him and was gratified to hear Marc's shout, and even more pleased to feel his cock spasm within her.

"Hurry up, Thad. I won't be able to hold on for long."

Hurry up? What was Thad going to do?

Before she could ask, Thad pressed against her back, the head of his cock poking at the crevice of her ass.

Surely he's not planning to…

Marc distracted her by gripping her hips and rocking her forward, the motion grinding her clit. She moaned and dug her nails into his chest. Again he did it, bumping the head of his cock, buried deep within her channel against her G-spot. With subtle swirls and thrusts, he kept her distracted, enough that she didn't protest the slick and oiled finger that probed at her rosette.

What a strange sensation, not bad exactly but different. Before she could decide if she wanted things to go further, Marc drew her down for a kiss. Tongue busy, she could only shudder as liquid dribbled against her back door. The added lube allowed Thad to pop a finger in.

"Oh." She couldn't prevent the gasp of surprise. The intruding finger seesawed gently, stretching her tight ring.

"Push out against it," advised Thad in a soft purr against her ear.

Willing to give this new experience a try, she did as told, and the pressure eased. Before she could make up her mind on whether she liked it or not, he slipped a second finger in. A second one should have made things worse, but to her surprise, the sensation went from odd and intrusive to…exciting.

With Marc's penis still sheathed in her pussy, and Thad's fingers pumping at her rosette, Toni found herself rocking in rhythm to their thrusts, her pleasure building again.

This appeared to be a signal. The fingers disappeared, and Thad's cock pressed against her rosette.

"Relax," Marc murmured against her lips.

He ground himself against her, reminding her of the pleasure. She pushed out, and Thad popped the head of his cock past the tight ring.

Oh, how stretched she felt. Stretched in two

directions. How could her body handle it? It was too much. Too—

Marc ground his cock deep, Thad sank deeper, their bodies covered her, and bliss blossomed. Shudders shook her as they filled her so completely. Quivers swept through her pussy, making Marc's cock throb, a throb that was repeated with Thad's cock. The guys began to move in rhythm; one sank deep, the other withdrew. Then the other thrust balls-deep while the other withdrew.

It was freaking insane. Yet incredible. The differing sensations somehow complementing each other. The friction of skin making her whole body tremble.

Lips found and latched onto the skin of her neck, a man for each side. They suckled as they filled her with their thrusting shafts. They nibbled as they drew her higher and higher. Her body tightened, and she couldn't help but bite at Marc, even as her lower body squeezed them. When her climax hit, they bit down, and she would have screamed if she'd not bitten down as well, the tempting flesh too much for her to resist.

Blood hit her tongue, and she couldn't help but swallow it. Marc's blood. His essence. His soul. All of it passed into her, through her, changing her, making her more, making her his, *making him mine*.

She felt not just with her body but with her spirit as Marc came, his cock jerking and spurting his seed. She felt his contentment, his and his wolf's, yet there was still another thrusting into her. Striving for the same peak.

Thad still sucked at his mark, and she felt him drawing at her essence, each tug jolting her pussy, making her climax roll over and over.

With Marc spent, she pushed up until she was on her hands and knees, rocking her body back, meeting Thad's thrusts, feeling his pleasure mount. He just needed one more thing. With his neck out of reach, she went after the one part she could get her teeth on. His arm.

She bit him on the wrist, a hard chomp that would leave a rounded mating scar, or so her wolf assured her. She tasted his blood, his sweet, rich blood. Ready for it this time, the freaky moment of joining didn't take her as much by surprise, but it was still just as intense. She came again, her whole body clenching tight as flashes of his life and emotions rolled through, the most predominant feeling being the love he bore her.

"I love you too," she gasped, unsure if he was getting the same flow of information and wanting him to know it.

With a yell of her name, not aloud but in her head, *Antonia!*, Thad came within her with a final thrust, and then he collapsed against her back.

And she collapsed against Marc.

Squished between her lovers—*No, my mates*—she smiled. For better or worse, she was bound to these two men. From hopelessness to love times two. No matter what the world brought her way, she wouldn't face it alone. Nor would she cower.

She'd found hope, courage, and love, and nothing, not even a freak intent on taking over the world, would take it away from her. Not if she and her mates had a say.

Epilogue

Days later…

Thaddeus surveyed his demesne, a house he'd never really shared, until now. And now? Now the place was overrun with vampires and wolves. Had he lost his mind along his tumultuous journey?

No, but he'd definitely lost his heart. Toni slid an arm around his waist and leaned her head against his shoulder. Through their bond, her love for him warmed and filled his heart—and his cock.

On her other side, Marc appeared, his stealthy abilities increasing daily with practice, enough that even Thaddeus found it difficult to spot him unless he cheated and used the thread that tied them together.

"A penny for your thoughts," Toni murmured.

He gave her the disgruntled truth. "How did I go from loner to this?" He gesticulated at the rescued wolves, a quad of them, sparring with Sasha in the courtyard.

Toni laughed, the sound so sweet he'd kill anyone who dared threaten it.

"You fell in love," she stated.

He sighed. "That I did."

"Do you regret it?"

Regret? How absurd! He glanced down at Toni, relieved to see no doubt in her eyes, just a smile at her serious, yet teasing comment. "No, of course not. I'll admit, though, the fact that I share my lifemate with a wolf is unprecedented. And strange. Not a bad strange mind you, but different."

"I'll say," grumbled Marc, but again, Thad knew this was more out of habit than any real dislike. Despite their differences, and perhaps because of them, the wolf truly was his friend. A best friend. And like any buds were wont to do, they bugged each other mercilessly. It drove Toni mental, which was a source of entertainment as well.

"If you ask me, this was meant to be," she announced, linking her hands with Thad's and Marc's, completing the circle.

"The three of us? Vampire and Lycans, in a happily ever after?" Thaddeus arched a brow.

"Yes. Don't get me wrong. I totally get we're not traditional in any sense, but that doesn't make what we have less. As a matter of fact, I think the fact we found each other and fought against habit and old, outdated ways makes what we have even more special."

"And what do we have?"

"A pack. A new kind of pack order. A pack for the future."

Her words rang out, and Thaddeus could almost see their impact, as if the mere saying of them changed something in the world. He already knew many wouldn't accept their unusual trio. Nathan and his pack had made it clear they were not welcome. The vampires he knew were keeping to themselves. But…Thaddeus didn't care. For the first time in centuries, he was in love. Happy.

And yes, menace still probably threatened. They'd probably have to fight—and kick some serious ass. But perhaps what they'd achieved was the first step to a new future. Let their new pack order show the way for all of them to find a way to live in harmony.

Or die if they tried to take it from him.

* * * *

The loss of Morpheus and the rogues turned ghoul was regrettable, but every war had its casualties. Of more annoyance was the missed opportunity to take the life essence of the one called Thaddeus.

How his power would have been welcome. But, in the end, it, too, wasn't needed.

War would come whether or not the vampire lived. Chaos would ensue, despite Thaddeus and his misfit group of wolves and minions.

Already the plan was in motion. It wouldn't be long now before blood was drawn and the gauntlet thrown.

A shiver of delight wormed its way along the spine. Soon the world would take notice. Tremble. And fear.

A new dark age arises. No longer will we hide in

shadows. The weak shall follow or die. And I shall be the one to lead them into the new beginning.

The End

www.ingramcontent.com/pod-product-compliance
Lightning Source LLC
LaVergne TN
LVHW012036070526
838202LV00056B/5519